P9-EEM-061

Walking on Ice

AWP 11

Walking on Ice

Stories by
Susan Hubbard

University of Missouri Press
Columbia and London

Copyright © 1990 by Susan Hubbard
University of Missouri Press, Columbia, Missouri 65201
Printed and bound in the United States of America
All rights reserved

5 4 3 2 1   94 93 92 91 90

Library of Congress Cataloging-in-Publication Data

Hubbard, Susan.
  Walking on ice : stories / by Susan Hubbard.
      p.   cm. — (The AWP award series in short fiction)
  Some of the stories originally appeared in various
periodicals.
  Contents: The sitter—My first dance—Belfast holiday—
The power of the great—Walking on ice—House guest—
Smoke—Dog—As good as it gets.
  ISBN 0-8262-0752-9 (alk. paper)
  I. Title. II. Series.
PS3558.U215W35   1990
813'.54—dc20   90-39139
                                                                              CIP

∞™ This paper meets the minimum requirements of
the American National Standard for Permanence of Paper
for Printed Library Materials, Z39.48, 1984.

Designer: Darin M. Powell
Typesetter: Connell-Zeko Type & Graphics
Printer: Thomson-Shore
Binder: Thomson-Shore
Typeface: Triumvirate

To my sisters

The AWP Award Series in Short Fiction

This volume is the first-place winner of the annual AWP Series in Short Fiction, sponsored by the Associated Writing Programs, an organization of over ninety colleges and universities with strong curricular commitments to the teaching of creative writing, headquartered at Old Dominion University, Norfolk, Virginia.

Each year, a collection of outstanding short fiction is selected by a panel of distinguished fiction writers from among the many manuscripts submitted to the AWP Award Series competition. The University of Missouri Press is proud to be associated with the series and to present *Walking on Ice* as the 1990 selection.

Contents

Acknowledgments   ix

The Sitter   1

My First Dance   11

Belfast Holiday   19

The Power of the Great   34

Walking on Ice   44

House Guest   59

Smoke   74

Dog   89

As Good As It Gets   105

Acknowledgments

I would like to thank Tobias Wolff and Raymond Carver, my professors at Syracuse University, and Thomson Littlefield, fiction editor of *The Albany Review,* for their encouragement.

Some of the stories in this collection originally appeared in the following: "Belfast Holiday" in *The Albany Review;* "The Power of the Great*"* in *The Dickinson Review;* "The Sitter" (as "Noise Out of the Dark") in *The Wooster Review;* and "Walking on Ice" (as "Winter Crossing") in *Passages North.*

Walking on Ice

The Sitter

"You've had plenty of experience with six-month-olds, I guess?" Mrs. Ellis stood in the center of her beige Indian carpet. Her hands were on her hips.

The sitter looked at Mrs. Ellis as if memorizing her. She looked especially hard at her hair, which was curly from a recent permanent, and at her lips, which were painted a deep shade of plum.

"Sure," the sitter said. She wore jeans and a dark blue sweater. The sweater had little balls of loose wool gathered along its sleeves and under its arms. She might have been a pretty girl, had she weighed sixty or seventy pounds less. But had she weighed less, she never would have been baby-sitting on a Friday night.

"You said you had references," Mrs. Ellis said. She knelt to pick up a baby bottle that lay on the carpet.

"You know the Bowens?" the sitter said.

"I haven't lived here long," Mrs. Ellis said.

The sitter turned her head away from Mrs. Ellis to stare at a teddy bear lying on the coffee table. Mrs. Ellis followed her gaze, trying to see the room as the sitter saw it, for the first time. If anything there was too much furniture. Her husband had said when he left, "You can have it all."

"My name is Elizabeth," the sitter was saying. "Not Liz."

"Did I call you Liz? I'm sorry," Mrs. Ellis said. She looked with longing at her favorite armchair, with the afghan spread across its seat. "Aspen is usually awake by now," she said, forcing her eyes away from the chair. "Her normal nap time is two o'clock. But today, I didn't get her down until four."

The sitter shrugged.

"I'd have liked you to meet her at least before I left," Mrs. Ellis said. "But if I wait any longer, I'll be too late." She

1

glanced at the grandfather clock in the corner. "I really do need to get out," she said.

The sitter was pulling bits of wool from her sweater. She rolled them into little balls and let them drift to the floor.

"You remember what I told you?" Mrs. Ellis asked suddenly. "About the diapers?"

"I remember," the sitter said, rolling another ball.

"Fine," Mrs. Ellis said. "The doctor's number is on the bulletin board by the telephone, just in case. And I'll be at the other number for an hour or so. If I go somewhere else, I'll call." She looked hard at the girl's face. The features were small, set close together, surrounded by puffy flesh. The skin around her eyes looked dark and slightly swollen.

The sitter breathed through her mouth, exhaling with a rasping sound.

Mrs. Ellis took a last look at the living room, at the row of mystery novels in the bookcase and at the love seat by the window. She made herself move toward the door. As she walked she tucked her ruffled blouse more securely into the waistband of her skirt. Then she picked up her purse and opened the front door.

The sitter stayed where she was, in the living room, pulling more wool from her sweater.

"Well, good-bye for now," Mrs. Ellis said. "When Aspen wakes up, she'll be happy playing here on the carpet. She won't mind if the television's on. She's used to it."

The sitter said, "Bye."

"Don't forget about the diapers. And help yourself to the cookie jar." Mrs. Ellis took a last look at the girl's face. The sitter's mouth opened, stretched wide, exposing dark-colored teeth and silver braces. Was she smiling?

"Good-bye then," Mrs. Ellis said. She pushed aside the screen door. By the time it hissed back into place behind her, she was halfway to her car. She didn't look back.

*   *   *

"I just got back from Florida," the lawyer said.

"That explains your tan," Mrs. Ellis said. "You look so healthy, compared to the rest of us."

She was chain-smoking mentholated cigarettes. The lawyer bought her another glass of wine.

"Are you a regular here?" he asked her.

"No. This is maybe the third time I've come in," Mrs. Ellis said. She had been in once before, for lunch with her sister. "I like to have a drink somewhere at the end of the week. It's nice to unwind."

"You like basketball?" he said, gesturing at the television set over the bar. He was what she thought of as a small man, compactly built. Her husband was six foot three.

"No. I don't really understand it," Mrs. Ellis said. "I was watching it for something to do." She knew she was saying the wrong things.

"What kind of law do you practice?" she said, determined to start again.

"Every kind," the lawyer said. "Civil, criminal, corporate. You name it."

"Divorce?" she asked.

"Yes, I handle divorces, too," he said. "Are you divorced?"

"Nearly divorced," she said. "Another couple of weeks and it should all be settled, they tell me."

"Who's handling it?"

"Bach, Lyman, and Cole," she said. "My husband has Pitman Bruce."

"It's a rough time," he said. His hair was brown, flecked with silver near his temples.

"Are you? Divorced?" she asked.

"No," he said. "No, I'm not even married."

"Not married," Mrs. Ellis said. "Ever?"

"Never," he said, watching her drink the wine. His eyes were light grey and had a serious expression.

"That's funny," she said.

"What's funny?"

"To be not ever married," she said. "I mean, you must be thirty-five or forty, am I right?"

"You're generous," he said.

"It's just that, past a certain age, nearly everyone gets married," she said. "It's almost impossible to avoid."

"Well, I did," he said. "Maybe it's an occupational hazard."

"Pardon?" she said.

He leaned back in his chair. "I've seen so many relationships come unstuck," he said. "I've handled divorces for so many friends. Nine out of ten times there's no big reason. It's the day-to-day stuff, trivia, really, that accumulates, and one day the sheer weight of it suffocates whatever love was there."

Mrs. Ellis took another cigarette from her pack and picked up her lighter.

"I won't light it for you," the lawyer said. "It's a deadly habit." Then he laughed. "See what I mean?"

Mrs. Ellis was lighting her cigarette. She shook her head, and turned away from him to exhale the smoke.

"It's an occupational hazard," he said. "I met you only minutes ago, and already I'm noting your bad habits. I'm too aware of these things."

Mrs. Ellis shifted in her chair. "I quit smoking for two years," she said. "Then last month I started again."

"Why did you start again?"

She sighed. "This sounds terrible," she said. "You see, my husband couldn't stand cigarettes. So when he left, I think I started smoking to get even with him. Does that make sense?"

The lawyer laughed. Then, abruptly, he finished his drink. When he put down his glass, he said, "I live with my mom and dad. They're wonderful souls, both in their seventies. Another?" he asked, touching her glass.

"Thank you," she said. "Excuse me for a moment. I must make a telephone call."

The telephone was on the wall at the back, near the rest rooms. The corner smelled strongly of floral-scented disinfectant. Mrs. Ellis put in a quarter and dialed. The sitter answered in the middle of the first ring: "Hello."

"This is Mrs. Ellis." She cupped her free hand over her right ear to keep out the noise from the bar. "Is everything okay?"

"Sure," the sitter said.

"Is Aspen up yet?"

"No," the sitter said. "No, she isn't."

"Heavens, I think you'd better wake her up then," Mrs. Ellis said. "Otherwise she'll never go to sleep later on."

The sitter didn't say anything.

"Hello? Are you there?" Mrs. Ellis said.

"Sure," the sitter said.

"Did you hear me? About getting Aspen up?"

"Sure," the sitter said. "No problem."

"That's fine, then," Mrs. Ellis said. "I'll see you later." The line went dead. Mrs. Ellis listened to the static. Slowly she replaced the receiver.

"Everything okay?" the lawyer asked when she returned to the bar.

"Yes, of course," Mrs. Ellis said. "I had to check in with my baby-sitter."

"How many children?"

"Just one," Mrs. Ellis said. "A little girl." She added, "I'm just a worrier."

"In headaches and in worry," the lawyer said.

"Pardon?"

"It's a line from Auden. 'In headaches and in worry, vaguely life leaks away, and Time will have his Fancy, tomorrow or today.'" He spoke the lines sonorously, then smiled with self-mockery. "Come along, madam, I'll buy you dinner," he said.

"I couldn't," Mrs. Ellis said. Then, afraid he wouldn't ask again, she said, "I couldn't, but I will." She finished her wine. "I like that poem," she said.

From the restaurant she telephoned the sitter, to say she would be back a little later than expected.

The sitter said, "No problem," and hung up abruptly, as before.

*   *   *

"I'd ask you in, but it's late." Mrs. Ellis said. It was after eleven when they reached her house. The lawyer had followed her home so that he could give the sitter a ride. He said, "I'll take the girl home for you. You wouldn't want to take the baby out, when it's so late."

Mrs. Ellis leaned forward slightly, her hand on the roof of the lawyer's car, to talk to him through the window.

"I enjoyed tonight," she said.

"Give me your number," he said. "I'll call you."

"I'm in the directory," she said. "Under James Ellis."

"I'll remember," he said. "I'll be in touch soon."

She said, "I'll just get Elizabeth." She walked briskly to the house, smiling. I can manage, she thought.

She turned the doorknob. The door was locked. She thought the sitter must be afraid of prowlers. She wondered why none of the other sitters had ever locked the door.

Mrs. Ellis knocked. She didn't want to waken Aspen with the doorbell. She knocked again, more loudly.

Behind her, the engine of the lawyer's car idled softly. Mrs. Ellis found her key in her purse and put it in the lock. When she turned it, nothing happened. The sitter must have bolted the door. Mrs. Ellis knocked once more. Then she rang the bell. She heard the chimes, muffled, through the door.

This is my house, she thought.

She hammered at the door with her fist. She pressed the doorbell again and again, listening to the chimes echo through the rooms.

The door swung open. The sitter stood inside. She looked over Mrs. Ellis's shoulder, toward the street.

"Where were you!" Mrs. Ellis said, her voice high.

"In the bathroom," the sitter said. Mrs. Ellis strode past her. All of the window shades in the living room had been lowered. The kitchen curtains were drawn. The rest of the house looked neat and ordinary.

"Did anything happen?" Mrs. Ellis said.

The sitter said, "It went okay."

"What time did Aspen finally go to bed?"

"Nine," the sitter said.

"Did you give her the bottle?"

"Sure," the sitter said. She was staring at the carpet.

"Were there any problems?"

"No problems," the sitter said.

Mrs. Ellis looked around the room again. She heard the lawyer rev the car engine outside.

"All right," Mrs. Ellis said. "All right. Let's see. You arrived at five." She glanced at the grandfather clock. "It's 11:30 now. That makes it—"

"Nine seventy-five," the sitter said.

Mrs. Ellis did some mental calculations. "Yes. That's correct," she said. She took out her wallet. "Well, let's call it ten, shall we?"

The sitter took the money. She held it loosely in her hand without looking at it.

"Now, Mr. Morrissey is going to drive you home," Mrs. Ellis said. "He's waiting outside."

The sitter's mouth stretched open briefly. Shreds of food were caught in her front braces. As she moved toward the door, her footsteps rattled the china in the glass-doored cabinet.

"Thank you, Elizabeth," Mrs. Ellis called after her.

The door slammed. Mrs. Ellis took a deep breath. She climbed the stairs quickly. The door to Aspen's room stood ajar. Mrs. Ellis stopped on the threshold and peered inside. It was too dark. She reached for the flashlight she kept by the door. The overhead light would waken the baby. She switched on the flashlight.

Aspen was asleep. She lay on her back. Her round head was white in the flashlight's beam. Her small hand was pink, curled against a blue blanket.

Mrs. Ellis took another deep breath and exhaled quietly. She turned off the flashlight and silently shut the door.

When the telephone rang she was in the bathroom, removing her makeup. Startled, she looked at her face, half-white with cold cream, in the mirror. No one ever called her late at night.

She ran to the upstairs extension in her bedroom. First she removed the receiver, then plugged in the telephone. "Hello?"

"Is Lizzie there?" The voice was thin. It must belong to an elderly person. Mrs. Ellis couldn't tell if it was a man or a woman.

"Do you mean Elizabeth? Why, no," Mrs. Ellis said. "May I ask who is calling?"

"This is her father," the voice said. "Lizzie said she'd be home by midnight. It's 12:27. Now, where is she?"

"Why, I don't know," Mrs. Ellis said. "She should be there. A friend of mine drove her home, and that was half an hour ago."

"Mrs. Ellis," the voice said. "Where's my daughter?"

"She left here half an hour ago," Mrs. Ellis said. "She must be there."

"Mrs. Ellis, you get hold of your friend," the voice said. "You find out what's going on here."

"I'm sure it's nothing," Mrs. Ellis said. "I can't imagine where she is."

"You call that friend," the voice said. "Then you call me. It's 12:28."

"Yes," Mrs. Ellis said. She replaced the receiver. For a moment she sat on the bed, looking at the telephone. The digital clock on the bedside table clicked to 12:29. She picked up the receiver and dialed.

"Directory assistance for what city?" a voice said.

"Boston," Mrs. Ellis said. "A listing for Patrick Morrissey."

"Address?"

"I don't have the address."

"We show no listing for any last name Morrissey, first name Patrick," the voice said.

"That can't be," Mrs. Ellis said. "He's an attorney."

"Ma'am, we show no listing for any last name Morrissey, first name—"

Mrs. Ellis hung up. Her hands were sweating. She was lighting a cigarette when the telephone rang again. She grabbed the receiver. "Hello?"

"Mrs. Ellis?"

"Yes, yes, is Elizabeth home?"

"No," the voice said. "No, she is not. What's the story on this friend of yours?"

"I couldn't reach him," Mrs. Ellis said. "I tried. There's some trouble with the telephone."

"Mrs. Ellis," the voice said. "It's 12:34, Mrs. Ellis. I've been waiting here since midnight. I'll wait twenty minutes more. Then I call the police."

Mrs. Ellis twisted the receiver cord around her fingers.

"Your friend," the voice said. "Who is this friend?"

"He's a lawyer," Mrs. Ellis said, her voice weak. "His name is Patrick Morrissey."

"I never heard of him," the voice said. "A lawyer, you say? Where does he live?"

"I don't know," Mrs. Ellis said.

"You don't know where he lives? And you let him drive my daughter home?"

Mrs. Ellis didn't say anything.

The voice said, "I'll wait twenty minutes. Then I call the police."

Mrs. Ellis pulled the receiver away from her ear.

The voice said, "You haven't heard the end of this."

*   *   *

She sat on the edge of the sofa in the living room, in the dark. She smoked cigarette after cigarette. The grandfather clock struck one.

Immediately afterward the telephone rang. The telephone was a wooden model, a replica of an antique, selected by her husband. She picked it up on the third ring.

A voice said, "Jane?"

"Patrick," she said. She sat down.

"I just wanted to tell you—"

"Where is she?" Mrs. Ellis said.

"Where is who?"

"Elizabeth!" Mrs. Ellis said. "The sitter! What have you done with Elizabeth?"

"I drove her home," he said. "What's wrong?"

"She's not home. Her father called. He's going to call the police!"

"Now wait a minute," he said. "Calm down."

"Where is she?" Mrs. Ellis said.

"Jane, I drove her home. I even waited while she went inside."

Mrs. Ellis tapped her fingernails against the receiver. She glanced at the window and automatically reached for the shade, to raise it. Then she stopped. She didn't raise the shade. She looked across the room, at the other window. She thought of the minutes she'd waited outside, pounding on the locked door.

"Jane?"

She let the receiver fall into its cradle with a thud. She went upstairs, directly into Aspen's room. She switched on the overhead light.

The baby hadn't moved. She was still lying on her back, half-covered by the blanket.

Mrs. Ellis drew off the blanket. Then, bending over the crib, she pulled apart the snap fasteners of the baby's pajamas. Aspen stirred and murmured. Mrs. Ellis ran her hands over the baby's shoulders, down her arms, over her belly, inside her diaper, down her legs. She turned the baby over and examined her back. The baby's skin was smooth and white in the bright light.

Slowly, Mrs. Ellis snapped up the pajamas. She switched off the light. She picked up the baby and went to sit in the rocking chair by the window.

She rocked back and forth. Through the window she could see the silhouette of the water tower on the hill and, past it, the lights of the office buildings downtown. The lights seemed to flicker in the darkness. She rocked back and forth. Aspen's eyes slid open. The pupils gleamed, dark and unfocused. Almost immediately her eyes shut again. Mrs. Ellis held her tighter. She listened to the baby's breathing. She watched the lights of the buildings. They made her think of stars.

From outside came the vague roar that was always there on quiet nights. It wasn't trains, or cars, or factory noise. And it wasn't the sea. It was noise that came out of the dark. It came out of nowhere.

Far away, the telephone rang. It rang and rang, as regular a sound as the baby's breathing, or the ticking of the grandfather clock downstairs. She listened as she rocked.

My First Dance

They called themselves "store boys." Every day after school they stood on the corner next to Ryan's Grocery and Mitchell's Laundry. Generally they stayed there until dark, talking and keeping an eye on who went by. Sometimes they made comments. Sometimes they had fights. All the girls knew they were there.

The store boys were at least two years older than I was, but I knew their names: Micky, John, Fred, Jamey, Pat Muldoon, and Pat McCarvey. My sister Edna was in classes with most of them, and she told me stories about what they did. She complained about the trouble they caused. She said they were stupid. But I caught her once after school, stopped in the middle of the sidewalk, looking into her shoulder bag with a funny pout on her face. I came up from behind and saw a flicker of light dance across the pavement. I figured it out. Edna had opened her compact inside her bag, and she was checking her reflection in its mirror before she walked past Ryan's Grocery.

But when Edna walked by, the boys paid no attention. Not even Micky, who whistled and moaned at every girl—even little rabbity Mary Francis McCoon, who had a terrible crush on Pat McCarvey.

Me, I was never sure which one I liked. John was tall and thin and blond. Most of my friends thought he was the handsome one, and I could see why. Micky also was blond, but heavier and tougher than John. He always had a black eye or a split lip. Pat Muldoon was the best fighter, and Pat McCarvey could imitate anyone's voice, even Sister Dolorita's. Jamey had dark hair. Some of it tended to fall across his eyes, and he brushed it back with his hand. His skin was dead white, but it turned red completely when he was angry or cold. He

11

was smaller than most of the others. He seemed to get into most of the fights.

It may be that I thought about Jamey more than I thought about the others. But I don't think I thought much about any one of them, until that Friday—the Friday that ended the first week of school.

The sun that day was hot enough to melt the asphalt on the playground, but the wind smelled like winter. I was walking home from school with Mary Francis. She said that a girl in our class was going to shorten her uniform to a length above her knees.

"Can you imagine?" Mary Francis said. "Sister Dolorita will never allow it."

I knew that she was right. I looked down at the plaid skirt of my uniform, which fell below the middle of my knee socks. The uniform was blue and green, and the only good thing you could say about it was that it hid ink stains. I wondered what I would look like in a short skirt.

"What would you wear to school, if you could choose whatever you liked?" I asked Mary Francis.

"I like our uniform," she said. "Besides, Sister says it's better when everyone dresses alike. Then no one can tell the rich from the poor."

"We're all poor," I thought, but didn't say it. Mary Francis's father had lost an arm in a foundry accident, and now the family lived on his disability checks. Still, my sister Edna said they had a good settlement when he lost the arm—enough to make them better off than we were. Edna said if only our father could lose an arm or a leg, we would be on Easy Street.

Mary Francis and I crossed the street. Ryan's Grocery lay ahead. Neither of us ever went inside to buy after-school snacks. To do so meant crossing the line of store boys.

We were afraid of them, I know that now. They never spoke to us. They talked among themselves, and sometimes they laughed. But we always knew that they were watching.

That day five of them stood there, some in front of the plate-glass window, others leaning against the brick wall. They wore white shirts and school ties with the knots pulled loose. Their blue blazers lay in a heap on the sidewalk. They all smoked cigarettes.

We walked quickly, not talking, and we looked straight ahead. I tried to walk without moving my hips. We had passed them when a voice called out, "Hey Kathleen. You going to the dance tonight?"

Amazed, I whipped my head around to see who had spoken. But the number of faces confused me.

"I don't know," I said, careful. It could be a taunt.

"Yeah, well. Take it easy," the voice said. Now I could tell—it was John.

I managed to smile. We walked on. My heartbeat was loud in my ears. John Clancey wanted to know if I would be going to the dance.

Mary Francis sucked in her lower lip and didn't say a word. Neither of us spoke until we reached Lakeview Avenue.

In a small voice Mary Francis said to me, "Well, are you going?"

"Going where?" I said.

"Going to the dance." She looked at me as if I were a different person now.

"Oh, I don't know. I haven't decided." I gazed at the trash cans in front of the Delaney house. "Are you going?"

"My mother would never let me," she said.

"I doubt mine would either," I said. We parted then, as friends.

But from that moment I was set on going. Before, I'd had no thought of the dance. My sister Edna didn't go to a school dance until she was fifteen, and Margaret, our oldest, didn't go until she was sixteen. A few of the girls in my class would be going. They were the girls who wrote boys' names in ink on their arms and had mothers who "weren't responsible," as my mother sometimes said—meaning mothers who were on welfare or had husbands who didn't live with them.

I didn't care about who else would be there. John Clancey had asked if I were going, and that was enough for me.

I moved slowly along Lakeview Avenue. When the wind blew I could smell sulphur from the lake, which was out of sight, down by the foundry. Lakesmell Avenue, they should have called it. The houses on the street were old and built close together. Most had three stories of wooden clapboards, and most needed paint. My sister Edna swore that she would live in a brick house when she got married. But the only brick buildings I knew were the school and the church and the foundry. Me, I liked the wood. Who would marry Edna, anyway?

A stray cat bounded out from a vacant lot across the street and came to stare at me. I tried to pet it but it ran into another empty lot, next to the McClennons. The lots were strewn with broken bottles. Sometimes when the sun set, it lit pieces of glass among the weeds. I could see the bits of glass from my bedroom window, glinting like emeralds and diamonds, waiting for me to come and collect them. Behind the vacant lots was the railroad trestle. Some nights the trains awakened me, but I liked their sound.

When I came in that day, my mother was busy with Bridget, the baby. I waited until she was finished.

"Some of the girls," I began, "are going to the school dance tonight."

My mother looked at me quickly. "Are they?" she said.

"Yes," I said. "And I wondered whether I could go along."

"Well," my mother said. "You're a little young for dances, don't you think?"

I said, "I think I am old enough."

She said, "Maybe. Maybe you are."

"Does that mean I can go?"

"I'll tell you what," she said. "I'll talk it over with your father. If he says so, you can go."

I ran up the stairs to find Edna. She was lying across her bed reading a magazine, and she said, "Go away. I'm busy."

"I need to know what the girls wear to the dance," I said.

"You're too young for dances," she said.

But I asked her again and again. And in the end she told me everything: what to wear, how to walk, how to dance, where to stand, and how to handle Sister Dolorita and the chaperones.

*   *   *

My father came in at 5:30. He was a housepainter at that time. He said painting paid better than work at the foundry, but Edna said it didn't. "He just won't have a boss standing over him," she said. "That man is better off working alone."

I heard him running water in the bathroom upstairs. Then he came down and drank his beer and read his paper until the supper was ready.

I helped make the meal. I don't recall what it was. Pork, probably, or brisket of beef, always with potatoes and cabbage. Normally I complained about the smell of the cabbage, but tonight I said nothing. My mother kept her eyes on me.

We sat down at 6:30. I sat next to Michael. He and I are left-handed. I cut my meat into smaller and smaller pieces. Michael was passing his plate for seconds. My father cut his meat clumsily because his hands were so big. No one spoke, except Bridget, who babbled to herself.

The dining room felt small and hot. The light on the ceiling shone down very bright, showing up the streaks in the painting of the Last Supper that hung over the sideboard. Margaret had painted it as her gift to my mother last Christmas. Saint Peter's face looked green and bilious, as if he had eaten too much cabbage.

Everyone ate rapidly except for me and for my father, who chewed for minutes on end. His napkin was tucked into his shirt front like a bib. Finally, he laid down his knife and fork, and I did the same. Everyone scraped their chairs out from the table. I carried plates through to the kitchen—but not before my mother gave me a look that meant she noticed the meat left on my plate.

From the kitchen I went to sit on the front staircase. I sat halfway up, where I couldn't be seen, where I could hear the voices from the front room. At first all I heard was Michael and Edna, washing the dishes.

Then I made out my father's voice: "And that is the end of it, Martha."

I knew that meant trouble. He rarely called my mother by her name. He usually said "you" to her.

She came out. I took three steps down to meet her. She put her hand on my shoulder. "Next year, Kathleen," she said.

I shook my head and looked at the floor. None of us could talk to my father on workdays. He came home tired and after his drink he was mean. I went upstairs.

My room was the small one that Margaret had before she went away to the convent. The blue and silver wallpaper had been left over from a paperhanging job my father did, and at the end of the room was a narrow window. I lay on the bed, hating my father and hating my mother for marrying him. I heard Bridget crying and the others clumping up and down the stairs. Edna's voice said good-bye as she left for the dance. I hoped that no one would dance with her. After a long time my mother came in to say good night. I pretended I was asleep. I hated them all.

There was no clock in my room. But I knew it was late when I decided to go. I put on the skirt from my Sunday suit and my best blue sweater. I stuffed my shoes into my book bag. Then I took hold of the glass doorknob. Gently, slowly, I turned it.

My parents were in the front room watching television. The television set faced the doorway, and its blue and white light flicked across the row of framed photographs on the side table. We all were there, Margaret and Edna and me, in our First Communion portraits. Soon Bridget would be up there, too, I thought—wearing the same dress. I hated those photographs. It was my job to dust them.

I heard no sound from my parents, but I knew they were settled on the couch as they always were, watching reruns until it was time for bed.

As usual, the front door was ajar; the lock tended to catch when it was shut tight. It would be open until Edna came in.

I didn't breathe until I was outside on the porch. I didn't even think until I was halfway down the street, and then I marveled at my luck. The air was cold. It smelled of ashes from the foundry. I had never been out alone when it was so dark. I felt full of myself, and giddy. I ran lightly down the block like a dancer, the cold wind in my hair and in my ears.

Before I reached the school, I heard the music. I recognized a song I had heard on the radio, but it sounded better now. The windows of the school gym were tinted blue. They glowed from the lights inside, and yellow lights shone over the front doorway. I had never seen the school like this. It seemed an exotic place, full of mystery.

A few parents were waiting in front of the school, near the curb. Waiting for their daughters to leave the dance, I supposed. I made sure they didn't see me. Across the street was Ryan's Grocery, and it was dark and deserted. I ran across and went to stand in the shadows by the brick wall where the store boys smoked. The broken beer bottles on the sidewalk glinted like amber in the streetlight. It was peaceful there. I had a good view.

Some boys were wandering around the school yard, talking loudly and laughing. Edna's friend Marie came out to her father to plead for an extra half hour. Her hair was tightly curled, and it took me a minute to recognize her. In the end she gave up, and she and her father walked away.

The music changed. Now it was a slow song. Two boys in the school yard mocked the lyrics, throwing out their arms and rolling their eyes. I pretended that they weren't there. Instead, I thought of the couples inside. Edna said the chaperones didn't mind how close a couple danced, as long as there wasn't any kissing or necking. The word "necking" made me shiver. I wondered if she had told me the truth.

I moved my legs in time with the music, trying to keep warm. I must have been there ten minutes or so when the double doors of the school burst open. The noise they made as they swung back was like a gunshot. A boy darted out. He turned and shouted something back inside. Then he turned again and came down the steps to the street.

The parents and the boys in the school yard watched him. One of the boys called, "Jamey!" That's how I knew who it was.

Jamey ignored his friends. He came across the street. He stumbled once or twice. He was talking to himself. As he passed under the streetlight, I saw his white shirt and a dark tie pulled loose under his blazer. His face was red. I thought he must have been drinking. But he looked very handsome.

He moved toward Mitchell's Laundry, swaying a bit, still talking to himself. I couldn't hear what he said. He paused beside the storefront. Then he lifted his right hand and drove it through the laundry's plate-glass window.

The glass shattered. It fell on the sidewalk with a delicate sound. Jamey yelled "FUCK" at the top of his voice. He held his hand stiffly in front of him. He took a few steps toward the corner. Then he raised his other hand. He brought it down suddenly, punching through Ryan's front window. "FUCK IT" he screamed.

I looked across to the school. But the parents and the other boys hadn't moved. They just stared.

Jamey headed in my direction. He held his hands apart from his body, as if he were carrying them, as if they weren't his. I hesitated only a moment. I stepped away from the wall and let him see me.

He looked directly at me. I waited for him to come closer. I could smell beer and sweat as he neared me. His hair had fallen across his left eye. He was breathing hard. Blood was clotting on the knuckles of his hands.

"Hi, Jamey," I said.

He came closer.

"I'm Kathleen Bradshaw," I said.

"I know," he said.

I looked at his hands, then at his face again.

"Want to walk me home?" I said.

"Yeah," he said. "Okay. Sure. I know where you live."

And that was our beginning.

Belfast Holiday

She met them Friday at a dance downtown. The band played mostly rock and roll. He came over to her at the start of a slow song. He said, "Care to?" She said, "Sure."

She gulped the rest of her drink. He took the glass and set it on a chair. She smiled at him. They moved onto the floor.

He put one arm and then the other around her waist. He was an inch or so taller than she. She rested her hands on his shoulders and let him steer her around the floor. His white shirt smelled of tobacco and sweat. Her best summer frock was crushed against her legs. They swayed to the beat of the music. She leaned back once to see his face. He pulled her close to him again. When the music ended, he said, "That was marvelous."

"Thank you," she said.

"I'll just get us a drink."

"Thanks," she said. "My name is Darlene. Darlene Hodgins."

"Martin," he said, nodding. "Now don't you move. I'll be back directly."

The band began to play again. She watched the dancers. Blue and yellow lights on the ceiling gave their faces a green cast. The room had no windows. The smell of cigarette smoke was strong. Darlene imagined that she was underwater.

Martin came back with two glasses. "Here we are," he said. "Cheers."

"Here's health," she said.

They drank. She noticed that he wasn't wearing a wedding band. He had thick, black hair. She couldn't tell the color of his eyes.

"Don't you come here often?" he asked.

"It's my first time," she said.

19

"Is it? Did you come with friends?"

"No," she said. "I'm here on my own."

"You wouldn't be from Belfast."

"Not me. I'm a Cushendun girl." She said it proudly.

The band's drummer broke into a solo.

"Sorry," Martin said, moving closer. "You said Cushendall?"

"No, Cushendun," she said. "But it makes little difference. They're neighbors, you know. Both quiet little places by the sea."

His face had a serious expression. "Have you been living here long?"

"It's nearly a year now."

"And how do you like it?"

"I couldn't say that I like the city. But, well, it's never so lonely here as home."

He nodded, as if he understood. "You must have a boyfriend now, a girl like you."

She smiled. "No," she said. "I don't."

"Come on. A girl like you?"

"No, really." She was blushing.

"Another drink?"

"I haven't finished this one. But you go ahead."

"No. I'll wait."

"How about you?" she said. "Is Belfast home?"

"I've lived here all my life."

"That's a long time." She said it to tease him. But he didn't seem to hear. He stared at something across the room.

"Look," he said. "If you don't mind, I'll nip across and get us two more. It's not so crowded now. Do you mind?"

"Not at all," she said.

He left her. She took a sip of her drink. With the backs of her fingers she touched her cheek, to cool it. Someone said, "Dance?"

She looked up and shook her head. "No, I'm with someone," she said. The words sounded good to her. "He's just getting us a drink. Ta anyway."

As the man moved away, she smiled. She pulled the skirt

of her dress away from her legs and shook it gently to take out the wrinkles.

Martin came back and stood next to her without saying anything. His eyes went from her to the crowd. "You're quiet," she said.

"Sorry. Just thinking. Thinking what a pretty girl you are."

"You're nice."

"I'm not nice. It's true. You are pretty, you know." His eyes flicked away again. "There she is. That's my sister."

A woman came out of the dark and moved toward them like a cat.

"Louise," he said. She wore tight black trousers. "Louise, this is Darlene."

Louise said, "Hello. I like the way you dance."

"You were watching us?" Darlene asked.

"Yeah. Me, I was dancing with a great mule of a man." She touched Martin's elbow. "I left my handbag there with your pullover. Let me just get them. Then I'll buy us a drink."

When she was gone, Martin turned to Darlene. "So now. Do you have work here or family?"

"I have family about everywhere," she said, smiling. "And I work at the Royal Victoria."

"You're a nurse?"

"No, nothing like that. I do the meal carts. You know, hand round the trays. Actually, I'm on holiday, as of today."

"Terrific," he said. "And are you living with your family?"

"With my Auntie Chessie," she said. "She's off in Donegal, just now, visiting my cousins. They've got a new baby. A girl."

"Now isn't that fine," he said.

Louise came back. She carried an enormous handbag made of black patent leather. "Darlene is on holiday," Martin told her. "Buy us something to celebrate."

Louise bought two rounds. By then the hall was clearing. It seemed the natural thing to Darlene to ask them back to the house for a drink.

"That's a fine idea," Martin said.

"We'd love it," Louise said.

Darlene warned them it would be a good walk.

Louise said "Me, I love to walk."

"Why not, in such fine weather," Martin said.

They went through the streets arm in arm. They had to stop twice at the barricades. At that hour traffic was light, and they went straight to the checkpoints beneath the arc lights. Darlene told the soldiers that they were going to her place. The second time she added, "For a drink."

The soldier said, "Mind if I come, too?"

They all laughed. It was a quiet night.

They reached Aunt Chessie's place without meeting another soul. It was a brick terrace house: number 42 Boylan Street. Four blocks off the Shankill. If you stood on that corner and fired a rifle down Boylan when the street was empty, that bullet would strike nothing until it fell.

Number 42 was the same kind of house as all the others on the street. Sitting room and kitchen were downstairs; two bedrooms and bath were up. The sitting room window looked to the street. It had lace curtains. A framed photo of Ian Paisley sat on the windowsill.

They settled in the sitting room. Darlene went to the kitchen and came back with a bottle of gin. They talked about work and about spending money. They finished the gin and three bottles of bitter orange. Later Darlene brought in blankets. Martin and Louise slept on the carpet.

In the morning Martin told her he had lied about things. He didn't drive a delivery van. Louise was not a schoolteacher. He had lost his job for taking people south, across the border. He hid them because they were wounded. And there were other things, things that meant he and Louise must not be seen for a while. They couldn't go to friends yet. There were reasons—

Darlene interrupted. "It matters nothing to me," she said. Then she was silent for a time. Finally she said, "It doesn't matter. I don't want to know why you're hiding." She stood with her arms folded, staring out the kitchen window.

Martin began to speak. She interrupted again. "You don't have to explain anything. I've got nothing against Catholics."

*   *   *

After breakfast Darlene cleared away the plates. When she finished, she said to the others, "Well, what shall we do today?"

Louise said, "I want to sleep."

"We can't come out, you know," Martin said.

"You needn't worry about the neighbors," Darlene said. "Aunt Chessie takes in a boarder from time to time."

"Me and Louise will not be seen," Martin said. He stretched his arms and yawned. "We could use a nap," he said.

"There's twin cots in my room," Darlene said.

"Aren't you sleepy?" he said.

"I never sleep in the daytime," she said. "Anyway, I can move into Aunt Chessie's room, while you're here. You shouldn't sleep on the floor."

She went upstairs to shift her night things into Aunt Chessie's room. Then she made up the cots with fresh sheets. As she worked she could hear them talking, the words muffled, Louise's voice as low-pitched as Martin's.

When she came downstairs again, they were sitting on the sofa. Someone had drawn down the window shade.

"I made up your beds," she said.

Without speaking, Louise picked up her handbag and headed for the stairs.

"I may go out in a bit to do the marketing," Darlene said.

Martin nodded. He followed Louise upstairs.

When they were gone, she went into the kitchen. She looked into the cupboards. They would need more milk for the morning. She sat at the kitchen table and wrote out a grocery list: milk, bacon, bread, tomatoes, eggs. Martin looked like he wanted feeding up. So did Louise.

From the direction of the Shankill came the sound of sirens. She walked to the sitting room and waited. The sound faded away. Darlene counted the money in her pocketbook and wrote a note: "Out to market. Back soon. Cheerio, Darlene."

Boylan Street was empty. As Darlene walked she swung the carrier bag she had brought. Another woman came out of a house, wearing a summer print dress and carrying a string bag, and Darlene nodded good morning. When they turned into the Shankill Road, they could see more than a hundred women, walking from shop to stall, asking questions about fish, fingering the Brussels sprouts.

Orange pennants strung across the road flapped smartly in the wind. Portraits of William of Orange were displayed in some of the shop windows, along with banners proclaiming, "Remember 1690." The wind was crisp, the day brightening, and the street looked like a carnival.

Darlene lingered over the shopping. When her bag was full, she stopped at a café and ordered a cup of coffee. As she drank it she stood in the café window and watched the crowd. The only men in the street were grocers and soldiers. She watched a grocer, festive in his white apron, slide tomatoes into a paper sack and twist it shut, all in one motion. The soldiers looked jaunty in their khaki uniforms and black berets. One, a young blond boy, was eating an apple, his rifle slung across his shoulder, his face pink and delicate.

Darlene finished her coffee and picked up her bag. On the street she saw no one she knew. But she noticed the words painted on brick walls she had passed a hundred times. On the wall at the corner of Boylan Street, someone had written in blue paint: "Fenians Get Out of Ulster." Beneath it was scrawled in child-like handwriting: "FUCK THE POPE." She was perspiring by the time she reached number 42.

*   *   *

When she let herself inside, the house was quiet. She put away the groceries. Then she walked aimlessly from kitchen to sitting room and back again. Finally she decided to have a bath.

Upstairs, she cleaned the tub and then ran the hot water. She threw in a handful of lavender crystals. On the shelf by the tub was an old eyecup holding withered rosebuds. The bathroom smelled of dead flowers.

She lay in the tub until she heard the creak of bedsprings. Every sound from the next room came through the thin walls. She heard Martin say "Oh!" and Louise say "Again." She looked at her legs, thin and white beneath the wavering surface of the water. She could hear the rhythm in the creaking springs and she could hear her own heartbeat. When she stood up, she felt light-headed. Carefully she stepped out of the tub.

She dried herself roughly, pulled on her dress and shoes, and hurried downstairs. She turned on the wireless, but the only station that came through clearly was broadcasting a church service. She switched it off.

To steady herself, she manicured her nails. Then she painted them with polish. Shimmering pink, they made her think of boiled sweets, like the ones her auntie had at Christmastime.

*   *   *

Martin and Louise slept late. They came downstairs long after teatime. Louise immediately lay down on the sofa, using her handbag for a pillow. She said, "Pity we've missed our tea."

"I can make an early supper," Darlene said.

"Oh, we're happy with bread and cheese," Martin said.

"Well, there isn't any cheese," Darlene said. She turned toward the kitchen. "You'll have to be happy with what's here." Her voice had an edge to it.

"Fine, fine," Martin said. Louise rolled her eyes.

Darlene heated tinned beans and sausages. Louise covered hers with HP Sauce. Martin told her the supper tasted terrific. "Really," he said.

Darlene looked at him for a moment.

When they had finished the food, Martin turned on the television set in the sitting room. Darlene brought out three bottles of ale. She plugged in the electric fire to take off the dampness. Martin and Louise sat on the sofa, Darlene in her auntie's rocker. With the window shade down and the smell of the ale, the room seemed a homey place.

Without talking, they watched a documentary about Iceland. After the program, Martin and Louise played pontoon with a pack of cards Louise fished out of her handbag. Darlene didn't know how to play; her dad would never allow cards in the house. Martin dealt very quickly. His fingers were short and wide. When his head bent over the cards, his eyelashes lay dark and thick against his cheek.

Louise was all points and sharpness, thin hair and narrow eyes and long, skinny fingers.

Yet, they looked right together.

Neither of them said very much. Darlene had to talk; the quiet made her nervous. "I was watching the children. They played outside all afternoon, and there's one wee boy with lovely red hair who never makes a sound. All he does is stand about and throw stones at the others. They never pay him any mind—except once, when one of the big boys pushed him and took away his stones. But the wee one never cried or said a word. He went off and filled his pockets with more stones, and then—"

Louise cut in. "Shut up now, will you Dar." Her voice sounded rough.

Darlene felt her face redden. She wondered if Louise were ill. Then she thought, still, she shouldn't talk that way.

"Bring us another ale, won't you?" Louise said.

"Those were the last bottles," Darlene said.

Louise threw down her cards. "Back in a tick," she said, and headed for the stairs.

While she was gone, Martin said, "Never mind Loulou. She grew up down the Bogside. She thinks she's seen it all."

Darlene nodded. "I had a cousin in Derry," she said. "She lives across the water now. All for loving a Catholic boy." She said it without thinking. Then she blushed.

"Was that one they shaved all her hair off?" Louise came back down the stairs, carrying her handbag.

Darlene turned to look at her. "No. But they stripped off all her clothes in the town center one noontime. It was girls that did it, girls she was at school with."

Louise sat down next to Martin again. "Deal me in, brother," she said.

Darlene decided to do the washing up. In the kitchen she ran hot water into a basin, all the while thinking of her cousin. A quiet sort of girl, Mavis had been. At Christmastime she had sent a card with a silver angel on it. "Greetings from London," she had written inside.

Darlene dropped knives and forks into the soapy water. As she washed them she hummed a tune. Then she sang the chorus: "No, nay, never, I'll go ramblin' no more."

"Is that all you know of it?" Martin called in from the sitting room.

"That's all," she called back.

"You've got it wrong, you know."

"Well, I was never one to remember the words to songs."

Louise came out to the kitchen, carrying her handbag. She even took it with her to the bathroom. "Be a pet, Dar," she said. "Go round and get us some more drink."

Martin was singing: "No, nay, never, no more. Will I play the wild rover, no never, no more." His voice sounded unexpectedly clear and sweet. Darlene wanted to listen. "Hush," she said to Louise.

Louise said, "Please now, Dar." But there was no "please" in her voice. She moved closer. Darlene noticed thin black lines around the rims of her teeth, as if the teeth had been cemented into her gums.

Slowly Darlene took off Aunt Chessie's apron and hung it on its hook. Louise said, "You're a real pal," and handed her a crisp new ten-pound note.

Still singing, Martin watched her walk to the door.

"I won't be a moment," she said.

The last light of the summer day streaked the sky. Darlene buttoned her cardigan as she walked. The smell of factory smoke was strong. The air felt dense against her skin.

A group of children came around the corner. Their faces were red and stained with dirt and sweat. They were going home from the playground. They were singing. Darlene recognized the melody first—"Clementine"—and then the words. It was one of the hate songs. "Who's your father, who's your father, who's your father, Bernadette? Never knew one, never had one, you're a bastard, Bernadette!"

The song stayed in her head until she reached the pub. It was empty, save for two old girls swallowing stout at a corner table. Darlene said, "Good evening," and they nodded. One of them wore an old straw hat trimmed with faded artificial flowers that bobbed as she moved her head. Pop music came from the wireless behind the bar.

The barman gave her the bottles. "Having a party, then?" he asked.

"No. Just me it is," she said. "Just me."

He shook his head. "Drinking all alone? A darlin' girl like yourself?"

She took the change without counting it. "Ta then. Goodnight."

"What's your hurry, love?" he was saying as she reached the door.

She hugged the bottles to her. The pub across the road was ablaze with lights, and she heard the drumbeat of the band playing inside. She smelled food frying and tried to guess whether the smell came from the fish and chips shop next to the pub or from the Chinese take-away at the corner. The chippie and the chinkie, the children called them.

A small man stood before the chips shop, swaying slightly, a stack of papers near his foot and a loudspeaker in his hand. His face was red and he smelled of strong drink. His voice boomed and crackled through the loudspeaker. It was impossible to understand what he said, save for the word "accord," which burst through the static like a curse: "Accord . . . bloody accord . . . accord."

A sudden rush of wind swept away some of his pamphlets. Darlene shut her eyes to keep out the dust.

It was always better when you came off the Shankill. The wind was never so strong amid the rows of council houses. Darlene's hospital shoes whispered along the pavement in the darkness. Her arms ached. She shifted the bottles. An army Land Rover without lights passed her and moved slowly down the block. From the houses came murmurs of television.

Children still played here and there along the street. Up ahead, two small boys sat inside a circle of streetlight near number 42. One of them was the wee redhead. The other had dark hair, but might be his brother. Darlene tried to see the child's face. He held a toy railway carriage. She saw something grey move along the ground at the circle's edge.

She shifted the bottles again. The grey thing moved out of

the light. Was it a kitten? She drew closer. Then it ran into the circle and she saw its snout. And that stiff tail, dear God.

"You boys," she said.

Her voice sounded thin. She cleared her throat and spoke louder. "You boys!" She came as near as she dared. The rat twitched and began to run crazily. When it stopped, its mouth hung open. It must be rabid.

"You boys come here and see what I have for you," she said.

The children watched her without moving. She turned and looked down the row of doorways. No one was in sight.

"Come away now," she said.

The dark-haired one said, "Why?"

The rat was panting. "Come here!" she said, yet they did not move.

She set the bottles on a neighbor's doorstep. Two bottles fell over and rolled together. She caught them and set them back from the edge. She was thinking, thinking of Martin. But he couldn't help. He must not be seen.

She saw an upended dustbin against the wall two doors down. Without thinking she ran toward it. She grabbed the bin and pulled it away, its hinged lid rattling after it along the pavement. The rat sat and seemed to watch her come. With a shudder she dropped the bin over the rat and quickly slid it sideways, clamping on the lid as she righted it. Only then did she look at the ground. The rat was gone.

The children hadn't moved. They stared at her. She carried the bin back to the doorstep of number 42. The rat made small movements inside. She kicked at the door, then smacked it with the flat of her hand, keeping her other hand on the lid. Finally the lock clicked and the door opened. She staggered inside, holding the bin ahead of her. The door slammed shut. She looked straight into Louise's face.

"My god," Darlene said. "Why didn't you open the door?"

Louise began to speak. Darlene shook her head. "Where is Martin?" she said. She set down the bin, but kept her hands on its lid. "Martin?" she called. "Martin!"

"Shut up! You've made noise enough." Louise took a step toward her.

Martin came slowly out of the kitchen.

"Help me!" Darlene cried at him.

Martin looked at the bin. "What do you want me to do?"

"I want you to get rid of it! The filthy thing."

He looked at her.

"It's a rat in here," she said. "Don't you know?"

Martin took his hands out of his pockets. "And you want me to get rid of it."

"He can't go out!" Louise moved between Martin and the bin. "Why in hell did you bring it in here?"

"I'm not asking him to go out! There must be some way he can do it. I couldn't leave it out there with the children. It's rabid!"

"Come on," Martin said. "How could it be rabid?" He smiled. Darlene thought it was the first time she had seen him smile. "Darlene," he said. "Find us a sack. Something heavy, like burlap." When she hesitated, he said, "Don't worry. I'll hold the bin."

She rummaged through the kitchen shelves. Aunt Chessie threw nothing away. Darlene found an old potato sack. In the next room Louise said, "How will you do it?" Martin said, "Never you mind."

"That will take care of it," he said when she handed him the sack. He laid it on the lid and picked up the bin. He moved into the kitchen. "Shut the door. Turn on the telly."

Darlene shut the kitchen door. Louise switched on the television. Light flickered and spread across the television screen. The pop singer Rod Stewart was breathing heavily into a microphone. Two tall blonde women in satin gowns stood behind him, making pouting faces.

From the kitchen came a thump and a long, high-pitched squeal. "Jesus God," Darlene murmured.

Then came a series of thumps. With each one the squeal became more piercing.

Louise went to turn up the volume on the set. The squeals and thumps continued. Louise looked bored. Rod Stewart stopped gasping and began to sing, hoarsely, long chains of sounds. Darlene couldn't make out the words. She closed her eyes. "The ale," she thought suddenly. "I must bring in the bottles."

By the time the song ended, the noise from the kitchen had ceased. Darlene opened her eyes. "Is it over?"

Louise switched off the set. "Yes, thank God," she said. "I never could stand that twit."

Martin opened the kitchen door and looked in. "I'll bring the bin and you put it back outside, Darlene."

She lifted the dustbin. It seemed much heavier now. She carried it outside and set it back in its place near the wall. The sky was entirely dark now. The children were gone. So were the bottles she had left on the neighboring doorstep. She had her hand on the doorknob of number 42 when she heard Louise say, "Mind your feet, Bobby! There's rat's blood on your boot!"

*   *   *

Rain beat against the roof when Darlene awoke the next morning. Gradually the sound grew softer. When it stopped she got out of bed. She put on Aunt Chessie's flannel wrapper and went downstairs to make tea.

In the sitting room she raised the window shade. Above the chimneys of the houses across the street, the sky was white. Darlene took her teacup to the sofa and sat down. As she sipped the tea, she counted out the days left of her holiday. It wasn't so bad, the others being here. If she hadn't met them she would be lonely, or spend all her time cleaning the kitchen. A soft thud came from the window. The palm of a small, dirty hand struck the glass. She went to the window and looked down, into the face of the wee boy with red hair. She smiled and waved. His face was entirely solemn.

She waved again. He batted the glass again.

She tired of the game before he did. Waving good-bye, she headed upstairs to dress. On Aunt Chessie's bureau she found an old photograph album, and she brought it downstairs with her.

She was turning the pages of the album when the sitting

room suddenly grew darker. Five or six faces pressed against the window.

"That's her," one of them said, his voice muffled by the window glass. It was the dark-haired boy of the night before. Next to him, the wee redhead pointed at her.

Older boys were with them. One of them shouted, "Here missus! What have you done with our rat?" He seemed as tall as Darlene.

Darlene stood up. "Look now, you boys," she said.

"Where's our rat!" the dark-haired lad said.

The one with red hair held a chunk of concrete with both hands. "Better put that down, now," Darlene said to him.

"Where is it?" the tall one shouted. He pressed his face against the glass. "Give it back!"

"Go away!" She swooped across the room and pulled down the shade.

They all began to shout, their voices shrill. "Where's our rat!" "Give us the rat!"

They rattled the front door handle. She thanked God that the door was locked.

"What's all this." Louise stood close behind her. She was barefoot, wearing only Martin's pullover. Her voice was a fierce whisper.

The children were pounding at the door. For a second there was silence. Then they began shouting in unison: "We want our rat! We want our rat!"

Louise turned and padded back upstairs.

Darlene stood in the center of the room. The voices settled into a monotonous chant. Each time they said "rat," someone kicked the door.

Martin appeared on the stairway, buttoning his shirt as he came down. "We'll have to go," he said.

Darlene felt tears coming. "No," she said, her voice quiet.

"You'll be all right," he said. She shook her head.

Louise came racketing down, her handbag bulging at her side. She went straight to the kitchen door. Through its window she surveyed the backyards.

"There's no one," Louise said. "Bobby, will you come!"

He walked to the door. Louise opened it, and they were gone.

The front window shattered soon afterward. Then there was silence. Darlene listened hard. But there was no sound from the house or from the street.

She went to the kitchen to get the broom and dustpan. Her legs felt stiff, as if she had walked too far the day before. Carefully she swept up the broken glass and the chunk of concrete that lay on the carpet. She stooped to retrieve the framed photo of the Reverend Paisley. It had fallen to the floor when the window broke, but it appeared undamaged. She stared at it, ready to throw it into the rubbish along with the broken glass.

But in the end she set the photo on the windowsill again, turning its smiling face toward the street. She could hear a siren now, headed her way down the Shankill. She stood for a moment and listened as the sound grew louder. Then she sat down on the sofa and waited for the soldiers to arrive.

The Power of the Great

When he first saw her, she was standing alongside the A9, the road between Aviemore and Inverness. She made him think of bad movies, the ones in which blonde hitchhikers were picked up by married men. The consequences were always dire for everyone concerned. Nonetheless, he slowed the car. She had a long, straw-colored plait of hair on each side of her head. He waited on the side of the road for her to catch up. A lorry trundled past, headed in the other direction. The driver stuck his head out the window. He bawled at the girl, "Go back home to your mammy!"

When she reached the car she was smiling. "Did you hear that?" she said to him through the window.

He felt embarrassed. "You do look very young," he said.

Her smile didn't change. She had full red lips and small square teeth, like a child's. "I'm going to Inverness," she said.

"So am I," he said. "Come on then." He opened the door.

The car's interior was clean. It smelled slightly of ammonia. He cleaned it thoroughly every Saturday. She put her knapsack on the floor and her feet on either side of it.

"You're American, aren't you?" he said. He put the car into first gear.

"Does it matter?" she said. Her voice was calm and sweet.

Again, he was embarrassed. "I have cousins in New York," he said.

She said, "I don't suppose I know them."

He'd been about to tell her their names. Instead, he switched on the tape player. The theme song from *A Man and a Woman* began. His wife had given him the tape for Christmas.

"My name's Dave," he said.

"Dave," she said.

He glanced at her to see if she liked the music. Her face was serene. She was watching the road ahead. But he thought she'd prefer some other kind of music. Folk music, probably. He could picture her at a "Ban the Bomb" rally. She had that look.

Dave lowered the volume on the tape machine. "Been over here long?" he asked her.

"Nearly a year," she said.

She looked at him briefly, then turned back to the road. They were climbing a hill. All around them were the Highlands, grey rock pushing through green turf. Up ahead, the ruins of an old stone cottage stood close to the road. He thought he might tell her its story—why it had been built, and why it had been abandoned. But as they neared it, she said, "There's the kind of place I'd like to live."

Dave looked hard at the cottage. It had no roof. The windows were empty holes, their edges black from smoke. Before he knew what to say, they'd passed it.

The girl said, "Who knows, it may have been a Druid temple once."

The rhythm of the taped music improved his driving. His steering was smoother. His gear changes were better coordinated. In the rearview mirror he could see a corner of his face—one brown eye, some dark-brown hair. He thought he looked younger than 35. His wife said he resembled the famous hairdresser Vidal Sassoon. Dave wondered if the girl saw the resemblance.

"The heather's late this year," she was saying.

"Not really," he said. "Give it another two weeks."

The girl sat without fidgeting in the passenger seat. She was wearing blue jeans, a white jersey, hiking boots. She looked healthy and clean.

"You're not afraid, travelling alone?" he asked her.

"No," she said. "Why should I be?"

"You hear stories," he said. "Women alone on the road. They're so vulnerable."

"It's quite safe," she said, "if your judgment is sound."

"Judgment is one thing," he said. "Physical strength is another—"

She interrupted. "What's really important is the right atti-
tude. I'm not looking for trouble, and I can sense it if someone
else is. I can choose whether or not to get in a car. I can tell.
Nothing's ever happened to me."

A Man and a Woman came to an end. The tape began the
theme from another old film, *Charade.*

"How long are you on holiday?" he asked.

"I'm not on holiday," she said. "This is the way I live."

Dave said, "How?"

She smiled. "Have you ever heard of the *I Ching*?" she asked.

He shook his head. She reached into her knapsack. She
pulled out a battered yellow book.

"Some kind of religion, is it?" he asked.

"Closer to a philosophy," she said. "But really it's a tool. A
tool to a whole way of life."

"A tool?"

She half-turned in the seat to face him. "I'll try to make it
simple. First you ask a question, any question. Then you
throw three coins. Some people use sticks, but that's even
more complicated. You throw the coins six times, and each
throw translates into a line. You with me so far?"

"D'you mean a line on a piece of paper?" Dave said.

"Sure. When you get six lines, you get a hexagram. The *I
Ching* lists all the possible hexagrams and interprets their
meanings. You look up your hexagram in the book and it
answers your question."

Neither of them spoke for a moment.

"I throw the coins every morning," the girl said. "The
hexagram tells me what to do that day."

"What if you don't want to do what it tells you?" he said.
"Does the *Ching* take revenge?"

She laughed. "I've explained it badly," she said. "It doesn't
give orders. And it doesn't operate on any causal principle—
you do this, or else. All it gives you is a picture of a moment.
All the little details that converge in the seconds that you throw
the coins. It's up to you to interpret it."

Dave said, "Really." She laughed again. He wondered if
she were flirting with him.

"Let me give you an example," she said. "This morning I got number 34: 'The Power of the Great.'" She opened the yellow book and flipped through it. He looked over at the book. Dead flowers were pressed between its pages. The margins were filled with notes written in black ink.

"The Power of the Great," she read. "Perseverance furthers."

"Furthers what?" Dave asked.

She ignored him and went on: "The hexagram points to a time when inner worth mounts with great force and comes to power. But its strength has already passed beyond the median line, hence there is danger that one may rely entirely on one's own power and forget to ask what is right."

"What does it mean?" he asked.

She kept reading. "There is danger, too, that being intent on movement, we may not wait for the right time. Therefore the added statement that perseverance furthers."

"Furthers what?" Dave repeated.

She didn't stop. "Thunder in heaven above. The image of the Power of the Great. Thus the superior man does not tread upon paths that do not accord with the established order."

"Sounds a bit conservative, this *Ching,*" he said.

"I disagree," she said. She closed the book and looked up at him. "To the contrary, the implications of the book are anything but conservative. For Westerners, they're absolutely radical. It's called the *Book of Changes,* after all."

Dave could picture her as a schoolteacher. "Are you a student?" he asked.

"We are all students," she said.

He thought, I asked for that one.

"What does it mean, then, that 'Power of the Great'?" he asked.

"My interpretation is that I won't travel farther than Inverness today," she said. "I'd been thinking of going on to Achnasheen."

"Nothing but sheep in Achnasheen, I would have thought," he said.

"There's a station hotel there, too," she said. "I used to work there."

"Where do you work now?" Dave asked.

"Nowhere at the moment," she said. "I only work when I need money. I live simply, so I can save most of what I make. This is my real work." She waved her hand at the knapsack, the yellow book, the passing countryside.

"Don't you get bored, just travelling?"

"How could I? Each day is entirely different. I meet new people, see new places. I'm almost entirely free. I could live this way forever."

Dave reached for the packet of cigarettes on the dashboard. The girl wrinkled her nose, he noticed, but didn't say anything. She watched him light the cigarette.

"Don't *you* ever get bored?" she asked.

"Sometimes," he said.

"You have a job," she said. "And a family."

"Yes, that's all true," he said. "But they don't bore me." It sounded false, even to him. "How do you like Scotland?" he asked.

"It's beautiful," she said. "Beautiful in a way that's kind of intimidating."

"I know what you mean," he said, glancing out at the countryside. "Barren."

"You're not from Scotland," she said.

"No," he said. "From Brum. Birmingham, you know."

"What sort of work do you do?" she asked.

"What *do* I do. I sell things. Liquor, specifically. To pubs."

"Do you sell wine?"

Dave said "No." He stretched his right hand back and lifted his jacket from the rear seat. He rested it across the gear stick. He pulled a business card from one pocket, a cardboard coaster from the other. He handed them to her. Then he threw the jacket into the back again.

"'David Brown,'" the girl read. "'Babycham.'"

"District sales rep," he said. "That's our new drink, on the coaster."

"'Make your next one a Pink Baby,'" the girl read. She looked at him. "Is it any good?"

"It's very nice," he said. "Babycham and grenadine. Very nice. If you like that sort of thing. Do you drink?"

"Of course," she said.

"I thought perhaps not, somehow," he said.

She smiled at him. "I love pubs," she said.

"Do you," Dave said. "You know, my first stop is just this side of Inverness. Nice little place, called MacKinnon's. Perhaps you'd like to come in with me and try a Pink Baby."

"Thank you," she said.

"You mean you'll come?" he said.

"I'd like to," she said. "It's nice of you to ask."

"Not at all," he said. He took the cigarettes from the dashboard again and eased another from the packet. He lit it and inhaled deeply. He was careful to blow the smoke out his window.

"You know, I think it's marvelous, really, to live as you do," he said. "No strings, no commitments. But surely you must get lonely sometimes?"

"I like my own company," the girl said.

"Not even a little bit lonely?"

She laughed, and he joined in, both amused at the wheedling note in his voice. "Oh, sometimes a little bit," she said.

"And what do you do when that happens?"

"I put out my thumb, and hope that someone like you will come along, I guess."

They smiled at each other.

The road was sloping downhill now. The first of the houses appeared, set far back from the road. Overhead, grey clouds hung low in the sky.

"Back to civilization," Dave said.

The girl turned to look. The houses were small and white, scattered in groups of two or three. Each had its own garden.

"Who lives there?" she asked.

"I've no idea," he said. He glanced at the toe of her right hiking boot. He tried to think of something more to say. An unusual odor, sweet and pungent, mingled with the smell of sheep blowing in from the hillside. Almost immediately he identified it. Tarragon. He remembered the name as clearly as the names of boys who'd bullied him at school. Tarragon. His wife had put it in a casserole once.

"Look out!" the girl said suddenly.

He looked at the road. He saw no more than a red striped shirt, a small arm. Just a blur. Then there was a loud thud, the steering wheel jerked in his hands, the car shook. His foot hit the brake. The car skidded across the road, onto the grass at the side. When it stopped, he still clenched the wheel for a moment.

"What happened?" he asked. "Did you see?"

She shook her head. Her face was pale. Her lips were pressed together tightly.

Dave stepped slowly out of the car. A streak of blood traced the path of the skid from left to right, across the asphalt to the grass. The blood was dark red. It looked surprisingly thick. He did not want to look at the front of the car.

He made himself walk forward. Close to the wheel he saw a small leg, ending in a canvas shoe, hanging, suspended somehow, from the car, just touching the ground. Dave walked closer. He saw the child's face. The neck was bent back. The eyes were open, surprised. The blood had come from the chest, which was pressed tight against the radiator grille.

Dave heard a shout from across the road. Beyond the roadside hedges, three small buildings stood close together. An old man had come out of one of them.

The old man walked fast. He stopped about ten feet away from the car. His face twisted as he stared at it. "Dear God," he whispered.

"Jamie!" A woman was standing on the steps of the house. Her voice was shrill. "Jamie!" she shouted.

The old man looked away from the car, as if he were ashamed.

Dave wanted to say something to the old man. "I never saw a thing," he said.

The woman was running now. She was small and stout. She had dark, curly hair. Halfway to the car, she dropped the towel she was carrying. She ran clumsily. Her eyes looked crazy. The old man turned toward her.

"He must have run right into the car," the old man said. Dave kept his eyes on the old man. The woman's scream, when it came, made him feel light-headed. He put out his hands, to steady himself. The woman stepped back, as if she thought he might touch her. She looked at the car. Her eyes blinked rapidly. For a moment it was quiet. Dave heard birds singing in the hedges nearby.

The woman's mouth fell open. "Murderer!" she screamed. "Murderer! Murderer!"

The old man put his arm around her. She shrugged it off. Then her shoulders slumped forward. Her hands tightened into fists.

"You be glad his father's not home!" she shrieked at Dave. "He'd murder you! He'll murder you! When he gets here he'll come and murder you!"

The old man tried to lead her away. She wouldn't move. "Jamie!" she cried again.

Dave swayed slightly. He looked around for something to grasp onto. He looked back, into the car. The sight of the girl in the passenger seat stopped him. She was leaning forward in the seat. Her mouth was open. Her eyes were huge. She was watching the child's mother.

He decided not to sit in the car after all. He stood there, shuddering in the light wind and the summer sunlight, until the police arrived.

*   *   *

Afterward it seemed to him that the whole thing had lasted only minutes. The policemen asked very few questions. They measured the skid marks on the road. Once they'd decided he was sober and hadn't been speeding, they seemed almost sympathetic. They wrote down his name and his next three addresses at bed-and-breakfast houses. They'd be in touch.

The police wrapped the child's body in a red blanket. They carried it slowly across the road, through the break in the hedges, and into his house, to await the coroner.

His mother had finally collapsed. She was put to bed at a neighbor's.

Dave sat in the front seat of the car again. His hands were shaking. He lit a cigarette. The girl watched him. She'd never left the car. One of the policemen asked her questions through the car window. She said she hadn't seen anything; it all happened too fast. They hadn't been speeding. She was an American student, travelling to Inverness to visit friends.

Dave finished his cigarette. He pulled out another and lit it.

The girl said, "We're free to leave now."

"Excuse me," he said. He reached across her to open the map compartment in the dashboard. He pulled out a half-pint bottle of whiskey. He inclined it toward her. She shook her head. As he drank, she said, "Do you think that's wise?"

"I think it's necessary," he said. He took another drink. She turned away and looked out the window. He had a third drink before he put the bottle back.

When he turned the key in the ignition, the engine started at once. He felt dizzy, almost sick. How easy it was, to kill a child and drive away from it.

The girl sat rigidly. Her body was wedged tightly against the car door. "You can let me off anywhere," she said.

He glanced in the rearview mirror. His face was streaked with dirt. His eyes were red. He could smell his own sweat and feel it running down his sides and back.

They drove past MacKinnon's pub without saying anything.

They didn't speak until they reached Inverness High Street. He stopped the car in front of a tea shop. A silver, three-tiered tray in the window was piled with scones and tea cakes. He pictured her walking inside, sitting at a white-covered table, ordering tea, opening the yellow book as she waited. Figuring out what it all meant. Asking the *Ching* what to do next.

"I don't guess we'll ever be able to forget this day, either of us," he said suddenly.

She was picking up her knapsack. She looked at him over her shoulder. "It's different for you than for me," she said.

He stared at her.

"After all, you were the driver," she said. "I was just an observer. Nothing happened to me."

"Nothing happened?" he said. "You were there!"

She smiled. "I was just an observer," she said gently.

"You were more than that!" he said. "It never would have happened if you hadn't been there!"

She stopped smiling. Her voice turned cold. "Whatever do you mean?"

"I mean that if you hadn't been there hitchhiking, if I hadn't picked you up, this never would have happened. The car would have passed those houses minutes before that child ran into the road." He heard his voice, deep from the whiskey. "That child would be alive now if not for you!"

"No," she said. Her eyes were frightened, but her mouth was firm. She looked little more than a child herself.

She sat there, the car door open, the knapsack on her lap. She shook her head. "No," she said. She got out of the car. "No. It's nothing to do with me."

He pulled the door closed. She stood on the curb. She stretched out her right hand, as if to detain him. He put the car into gear. As he pulled away, she shouted, "It was an accident!"

When he last saw her, reflected in the rearview mirror, she was still standing there, shouting.

Walking on Ice

When Barry invited her north for the three-day holiday week-end, her first apprehension was that they wouldn't come home again.

They would be snowed in, she felt sure. Or the ice on the river would melt in a sudden thaw, and they would be stuck, marooned on his friend Donald's island.

Barry said she was silly. No way would they be marooned. The season was too late for heavy snow. And no way could the ice melt in three days. But say it did. Say, for instance, that the earth's orbit took a severe and unprecedented lurch toward the sun—well, they would simply launch one of Donald's boats and paddle their way back to the mainland. No big deal. One way or another, they would be back in plenty of time for school on Tuesday.

"I should stay home and grade papers," Mary said.

Barry pointed out that Mary had been grading papers all winter. Between grading papers and dating William Todd, the school psychologist (and being dumped by William Todd, who fell for the new kindergarten teacher, for Christ's sake), Mary's life had segued from the mundane into the melancholy. Barry repeated the last phrase, obviously proud of it.

"A walk on the ice is just what the doctor ordered," he told her, as they sat over plates of baked ziti in the teachers' lunchroom. "Put some fresh air into your lungs."

Barry was president of the teachers' union local. He didn't stop talking until she said yes.

"I can sell anyone on anything," he said when she gave in.

She didn't tell him that the deciding factor was her own determination to resist a desire to spend the weekend in bed, reading until she forgot herself—and William Todd.

They set out on Saturday morning in Barry's Volkswagen.

The back seat was crammed with sleeping bags, knapsacks, jackets, and Mary's briefcase, full of ungraded papers. They crossed the Newburgh Bridge and headed north. Mary felt barely awake, but nervous. Barry smoked little cigars. He did all the talking.

For a while he played at psychoanalyzing Mary. She obviously had a thing for her father, he said. He compared her life to various Greek myths and fairy tales, and recommended titles of helpful books. When she did not respond, he said, "Well, it's your life." Then he began to talk about Donald.

"He's my best friend, I suppose," Barry said. "My oldest friend, anyway. We grew up together. Every summer I'd be invited up to the island to spend a week or two with his family. That old house is gone now."

"What happened?" Mary asked politely.

"Fire," Barry said. "The place burned to the ground about five years ago. Those old houses are like dry tinder, just waiting for a spark." He smiled, as if the thought pleased him somehow.

"Where will we be staying, then?" Mary asked.

"We'll be in the place Donald built," Barry said. He lit another cigar. "He built it with the royalties from his book."

Mary watched cigar smoke curl across the windshield. "What book?"

"I don't remember the title. It came out when he was just twenty-two. He hasn't published anything since. It got reviews that were pretty incredible. They even made a film out of it."

"You don't remember the name?" Mary asked.

"Something with *It* in the title. *Leaving It Behind,* or *Getting Rid Of It.* Something like that."

"I don't think I saw the movie," Mary said.

"Nobody has. Some little outfit in the city did it. Artsy. Nobody's ever heard of it."

The Volkswagen pounded along the interstate. The car didn't have shocks. The road wound through the Catskills. Mary watched fenceposts, black against snow-covered fields, seem to revolve as the car went past. They had been driving for hours.

"How much farther?" she asked.

Barry rolled down his window a few inches and threw out his half-smoked cigar. "Next exit is ours," he said. "Glad you came?"

Mary looked at the dashboard ashtray, brimful with cigar butts. "Of course," she said.

Barry downshifted as they approached the exit sign. A truck swung out of the lane behind them and passed, the driver steadily sounding his horn.

"What's the matter?" Mary asked, startled.

Barry steered the Volkswagen down the exit ramp. "I think I'm falling in love," he said, half-singing the words.

Mary stared at him. "I thought you were my friend," she said.

*   *   *

They said no more until they had reached the town. They passed a high school, a bowling alley, and two car dealerships. "Where is the river?" Mary asked.

Barry did not reply. The car moved beneath an archway that read "Welcome to the Thousand Islands," then stopped against the curb.

"There's the river," he said, pointing across the street.

They pulled their jackets from the back seat and left the car. Mary looked where he had pointed, but all she saw was a field of snow. The air smelled of nothing—it seemed absolutely pure, like ice.

Barry led the way to the edge of the field. The wind rolled across the whiteness, stinging their faces. Mary's hair whipped across her eyes. She pulled a woolen hat from her pocket and pushed her hair inside it.

"Those are the islands," Barry said. Some distance away lay what looked like huge clumps of snow, with trees growing out of them.

"Which one is Donald's?"

"Down there." He pointed at a smudge of black and white, trees and snow, far across the ice and lying to the west of them. "It's called Champagne Island on the charts," he said.

"I like champagne," she murmured.

He put his left arm around her shoulders and pulled her toward the road again. "I'll buy you a drink at Marie's," he said. "That's where Donald will meet us."

They walked down the block, not quite in step. Briefly Mary looked sideways at him, noticing the unfamiliar smell of his leather jacket. Most of the storefronts they passed were empty. Everything seemed closed for the season. Only one building had a lit neon sign, spelling out "MARIE'S CAFE Cocktails Fine Food." It was next door to "MARIE'S MOTEL."

Inside, the café was dimly lit and stuffy, like a closet full of old clothes. Barry led the way between a pool table and a battered upright piano.

"You must have been here before," Mary said, taking off her jacket.

"Tell you what," Barry said. "Order me a scotch and water. I'll move the car into a parking lot for the weekend."

Mary said, "Right." Her eyes were adjusting to the darkness. She could make out the bar, and the figures of men drinking at it.

Barry left. Mary went to talk to the bartender, a woman in her thirties, wearing pink lipstick and a pink sweater. Mary ordered the drinks. The bartender did not meet her eyes. An old man drinking to her right ignored her; to her left, a group of younger men was watching. She glanced at them. They were in their twenties, dressed in plaid flannel shirts and jeans. Two of them had hair long enough to reach their shoulder blades.

Mary carried the drinks back to a table near a wall. The walls were decorated with dead fish mounted on plaques. One of the fish had teeth that looked sharp as needles. This, she saw from the engraved brass label, was a "Muskie."

Mary sipped her drink. The old man wasn't talking. The young ones were loud.

"Never again, never again," one of them said.

"Not since you fell in, huh?" another one said.

"Not unless I had someone to spend the winter with," the first one said. He turned to look briefly at Mary. She stared at the fish.

"Plenty of women on Grindstone already," one of the others said.

"Only in the summer," the first one said. He was tall and lean, with long dark hair worn in a pony tail. "Very few ladies want to spend the winter shut in," he was saying. "Now, this year I got my apartment right in town, with the grocery store right down the street. And I got Marie."

"Right you are, honey," the bartender said. She took his glass and refilled it with draft beer. "Rick is my honey," she said, to no one in particular.

"That was a terrible thing," the old man said suddenly. "Drove his brand new Dodge pickup right through the ice."

"That was ten years ago," Rick said. He sounded disgusted.

"Who they talking about?" one of the others asked. "Rick's uncle, that was," the bartender said.

"What was he doing out there in a truck?"

"He was ice-fishing," Rick said.

"It was a terrible thing," the old man said.

They stopped talking. Mary wondered what was keeping Barry. She drummed her fingers on the table and wished she had her briefcase. She had forty essays to grade before Tuesday.

The man called Rick went off through the door marked "Gents" at the rear of the room.

"Guess that was the last time he went ice-fishing," one of the young men said.

"Who? Rick?"

"Naw, his uncle."

The old man said, "His uncle was drowned."

"Probably froze before he drowned."

"They never did find the body," the old man said.

"What's the fishing like this year, anyway?"

Mary stopped listening. Barry was taking a long time to park a car. She looked out the nearest window, but all she could see was the motel next door and the cracked blue cement at the edge of a swimming pool in its front yard.

The old man set a pile of change on the bar and walked out, not saying good-bye to anyone.

Mary glanced back at the fish mounted on the walls. Their scales were stiff and shiny, as if they had been varnished.

"Your friend stand you up or what?" Rick was leaning over her table.

"I don't think so," Mary said. "Of course not."

"You staying around here?"

"For the weekend," Mary said.

"You at the motel?"

"No, with a friend," she said.

"Your friend like parties? We're having a hot one tomorrow night. Jody's coming out of the Navy."

"That sounds nice," Mary said, not sure if it did. "But we'll be on the island then."

"You going across the ice?" He said it as if he didn't believe it.

She disliked so many questions. "Yes, we're walking across," she said.

"First time?"

She looked sharply at him and saw from his eyes that he was teasing her. Before she could say anything, the front door opened. Barry came in, followed by a man wearing a green watch cap, both carrying two bags of groceries.

"Well, it's Donald Morgan," Rick said, looking at the man with Barry. "The old grey cat himself."

"Yes, it's me," the man said. He set the grocery bags on a chair. Then he unzipped his nylon parka and pulled off his hat. His hair was blond and curly and looked as if he cut it himself. He wore rimless spectacles and he pulled these off next. His eyes were dark blue, and they immediately focused on Mary.

Barry introduced them.

"Hi Mary," Donald said. He sat down at the table.

"Hello," she said.

Barry put his grocery bags on another chair and sat down.

"Oh, Barry, this is Rick," Mary said quickly. Rick smiled, and Mary realized that he had never told her his name.

Barry nodded at Rick, then picked up the glass of scotch waiting for him. He took a sip.

"Beer is fine for me," Donald said.

Barry looked at him. Donald didn't move. "Allow me," Barry said. He got up and went to the bar.

Rick remained standing by the table, his hands in his jean pockets. "Heard you're over on Champagne again," he said to Donald.

"Yes," Donald said. He rubbed the lenses of his spectacles against the sleeve of his sweater.

"You catching anything?" Rick's voice was nonchalant.

"Only colds," Donald said. "I only eat saltwater fish," he added, looking at Mary.

"How's Jennifer?" Rick said.

Donald stared down at his lenses. "Jennifer's back in Boston," he said.

"Walked out on you, huh?" Rick winked at Mary.

"Jennifer's living with her mother," Donald said. He put on the spectacles, hooking them over each ear.

"Couldn't take another winter, I guess." Rick lowered himself into a chair at the next table.

Donald turned to Mary. "Barry says this is your first trip north."

"I was here once when I was a kid," Mary said, happy to talk. "My parents took me on a boat tour."

"Probably went right past Champagne," Donald said. Barry returned with the drinks. "The old tour boats went further upriver then than now," he said. "Remember, Barry?"

"They went right by your front door," Barry said, sitting down.

"We'd be skinny-dipping off the dock, and the boat would come by, loaded with tourists and cameras, and the guide telling them the family history over the loudspeaker." Donald picked up his beer and drank half of it.

"Maybe that's why they changed the route," Rick said. He rocked his chair backward, balancing it on its rear legs.

Mary said, "How long has your family lived there?"

"My grandfather bought it in 1890 or thereabouts." Donald smiled at her.

"Tell her about the dead bodies buried over there," Rick

said. He let his chair fall forward and its legs hit the floor with a thud.

"Bodies?" Mary said.

"Soldiers," Donald said. "During the Revolutionary War. Supposedly died of cholera. But that's enough history. This is boring you."

"I'm not bored," Mary said. "History is my subject, you know."

"Drink up!" Barry said, looking at Donald. "You, too, Mary. Let's get warm before we get cold."

Rick pointed at Mary's boots. "You could have trouble with those," he said.

She glanced down at them—flat-heeled boots, made of suede and lined with sheepskin.

"Your feet are going to get wet," Rick said.

"Probably right," Donald said, his voice lazy. He had finished his beer.

"How far is it?" Mary asked.

"A couple of miles."

"How are we going to carry the groceries?" she asked.

"I have a sled," Donald said. "Don't worry."

"Whose round is it?" Barry slammed down his glass, and the bartender said "Careful!"

"Your round," Donald said. "I spent all I had on the food." Barry went back to the bar.

"Too bad about Jennifer," Rick said. "She was a nice girl."

"She wasn't when she left," Donald said, his eyes on the floor.

"I remember she told me she was painting a lot of pictures over there," Rick said.

Donald looked up. "Told you? Told you when?"

"Sometime when I ran into her. Sometime at the post office or some place." Rick rocked back in his chair again.

"She painted a lot," Donald said. "Didn't finish much. All she did was self-portraits, with layers and layers of paint."

Barry came back with more drinks. Mary drank down her second Bloody Mary to make way for the third.

Donald watched her. "You do any painting?" he said.

"I can't draw a straight line," she said. "I'm the opposite of an artist."

"Thanks be for that," Donald said.

Barry rested his arm on Mary's shoulder. "How about a little music?" he said.

"Later," Donald said. "My fingers are stiff."

"No, I didn't mean the piano. I meant the jukebox."

"Go right ahead," Donald said. "By all means."

Barry pushed his hand into his pocket. "Here you go," he said to Mary, handing her an assortment of change. "Choose us a song."

"Yes, sir," she said. He looked surprised at the tone of her voice.

Mary went over to the jukebox. The songs were listed on strips of pink and white paper beneath a fly-specked plexiglass cover. "Your Cheatin' Heart"; "Do It To Me One More Time"; "Another One Bites the Dust." She sensed that the men at the bar were watching her. Quickly she slid in the quarters. She pressed the red buttons, encoding "Let It Bleed" by the Rolling Stones and "Piece of My Heart" by Janis Joplin. She went back to the table.

Barry and Donald had been talking, their heads close together. They moved apart as she sat down. Rick, lying back in his chair, rolled his eyes at her.

"Have a match?" Donald asked her.

"What?" she said.

"Never mind." Donald stood up and went to the bar.

From the jukebox came a loud hiss, then the opening chords of "Another One Bites the Dust."

"You play this?" Barry asked. She shook her head.

Donald was talking to the bartender. She smiled at him, the way a young girl would smile at the school's best football player.

"Hadn't we better get started?" Mary said. "Aren't we going to cross the ice before dark?"

"Plenty of time. Relax." Barry tapped his foot in time to the music. "This is the first time I've seen Donald for many months."

"You ain't missed much," Rick said.

Barry looked hard at him.

"He tore up half the town dock last fall," Rick said. "Went out there in Joe Putnam's cigarette boat when he was drunk and stoned and came in doing more than fifty. Rammed the dock and a nice old Chriscraft, belonged to some Canadians."

Barry's eyes stayed on Rick.

"Then in October he got into a fight at Cameron's Diner," Rick went on. "Took off part of a guy's ear."

"Look," Barry interrupted. "Why don't you keep your mouth shut about that stuff?"

Rick inclined his head as if he agreed. Then he said, "Fuck you," stood up, and went back to the bar.

Barry's face turned red.

"Oh, God," Mary said.

Donald was drinking beer at the bar, still talking to the bartender. She was laughing as she listened. She had on earrings shaped like little bells, and they tinkled when she laughed.

At the bar's other end, Rick sat with his friends, and they all watched Donald.

Donald whispered something to the bartender. She shook her head merrily.

"Donald!" Barry said. "Don't you think it's time we made a start?"

Donald was smiling. "I do indeed," he said. "But first I've got to give these people a tune."

He walked quickly to the piano and set his beer on top of it, next to a tarnished trophy in the shape of a leaping fish. He flipped up the keyboard cover and ran his fingers over the keys.

The bartender pulled the plug on the jukebox.

Donald played ragtime tunes. Mary had never heard them before. The music was melodious, but Donald played at a furious tempo, his hands tensed, his neck bent over the keyboard.

He played for seven or eight minutes, and when he stopped, one of Rick's friends hollered, "All right!" The bartender and Barry applauded, and Mary tried to look enthusiastic.

But Donald paid no attention. He shook his head, looking at the keyboard. He played a scale, then played it again, running his fingers rapidly up and down the keys. Finally he slammed down the cover. "Get the damned thing tuned," he said to the bartender.

She looked as if she might cry.

Donald came back to the table and picked up his parka. "Are we going or what?" he said.

Mary stood up and reached for her jacket. Barry had buttoned his jacket already and was waiting at the door. As she pushed her arms into the sleeves, Rick came and held the jacket to help her.

"You sure you want to go?" he said, his mouth close to her ear.

His closeness startled her. His breath was warm and smelled of beer and cigarettes. Before she could answer, Donald patted her shoulder and said, "Ready?"

She nodded. Barry and Donald picked up the bags of groceries, then stood back to let her go first. Without speaking the three of them left the café and crossed the street.

Donald's sled leaned against the side of one of the riverfront buildings. Its sides were steep enough to contain the knapsacks, sleeping bags, groceries, and Mary's briefcase. Donald pulled the loaded sled toward the place where the ice began.

When he reached the river's edge, he stopped and took a coil of rope from the sled. He wrapped one end around his waist and tied it. Then he wound the rope around Barry and made it fast. "You can do Mary," he said.

Barry took the end of the rope and came up close to her. "I'm sure I'll be all right without it," she said. Her voice sounded small.

Barry didn't answer. He thrust the rope around her midriff and knotted it.

Donald pulled his parka hood over his green cap. "All set?" he said.

"Set," Barry answered. He took a wool cap from his pocket and pulled it on. Mary had never seen him wear a hat before. He reminded her of a circus clown.

"What are you looking at?" Barry said. He pulled the hat over his ears.

Donald picked up the sled's towline and stepped onto the ice. Snow had begun to fall lightly, and the dark shapes of the islands were indistinct. Barry came next, and Mary followed, wondering why she was last. They walked single-file into the white air.

Mary thought, at least it isn't slippery.

The snow wasn't deep enough to make walking difficult. For a while they followed a path beaten down by others. The wind died, and the only sound was their boots crunching the snow. Up ahead, the severed top of a small pine tree leaned to one side, stuck in a pile of snow. The tree must be a trail marker, Mary thought. When Donald reached it, he turned off to the left. The path of beaten snow curved away to the right.

The going was harder now. The wind came up again, making a hollow, humming sound that began miles and miles away from them, growing louder as the cold air swept over the ice. Mary could hear the men breathing.

She had no sense of distance or time. The islands remained dim shapes ahead, seeming no closer than before.

Mary wanted to look over her shoulder, to see how far they had come. But she was afraid that she'd lose the pace, tauten the rope, make the others stop. They walked with their heads bent forward. They never looked back.

From a long way off there began a loud creaking, an eerie, low-pitched sound that seemed to travel toward them from under the ice.

"What's that?" Mary shouted.

Donald stopped and turned around. Barry kept walking until he had caught up with Donald.

"That's the sound the ice makes as it settles," Donald said. His face, framed by the fur-lined parka hood, was red. A drop of moisture hung from his nose.

Barry turned and faced her, too. He had wound his scarf over his mouth and pulled his wool cap low, so that only his eyes and his nose were visible. He said something, but the scarf muffled his words.

"I can't hear you." Mary walked closer to them.

Barry said, "Scared?"

Mary smiled at him. The skin around her mouth felt stiff.

"Your turn," Donald said, handing the sled's towline to Barry.

They set off again. Mary had wanted to ask, "How much farther?" But Barry had made that impossible. She glanced at Barry's feet, noticing that he walked with his toes turned out. She kept her eyes on his feet. They looked smaller than hers, almost dapper in their shiny black boots. She adjusted her pace to keep the perfect distance between them.

Suddenly Barry's feet came together and stopped. Mary looked up. About thirty feet ahead, the ice appeared to have buckled. It lay in a thick ridge, curving upward. Against the ridge moved a snake-like thread of black water. Beyond the water the ice began again, stretching perhaps half a mile farther, to the base of an island—a white mound with black trees on top of it.

They all stared at the water.

Donald's voice rang out. "You can see the house now." He pointed with his nylon mitten.

"You can see something else, too." Barry's voice was so loud that the words carried easily through his scarf.

Donald beckoned them closer. Mary walked up to Barry. He didn't move.

"It's only two or three feet across," Donald said. "We can jump it easily."

Barry's eyes looked black under his red hat. He smelled of scotch and sweat and cigars. "No way," he said.

Donald walked back and stood across from them. "Hey, come and look at it," he said. "It's not as bad as you think."

Barry let the sled's towline drop. "How the hell do you know how bad it is?" he said. "How do you know what it's like on the other side?"

"Barry, I do this twice a week." Donald's voice was quiet.

Barry glanced down at the sled. "What about the groceries?"

"We could toss them over." Mary said it impulsively.

Barry's eyes glittered. His mouth seemed to move beneath the scarf, but no words came out.

Donald took a few steps toward the water. "It's a snap," he said. "Come and see for yourself."

Mary moved forward. But Barry stayed where he was. He looked from Donald to Mary. Then he removed his gloves. He came up to Mary and reached for the rope around her waist.

"What are you doing?" she asked.

He didn't answer. When he'd finished untying her, he went to work on the knots that held the rope around himself. Finally he stepped out of a loop of rope. He threw the slack line toward Donald.

"Mary and I are going back," Barry said. "You're welcome to join us."

Donald shifted from foot to foot. "Barry," he said. "Watch." He walked up to the sled and stooped over it. When he straightened up, he had two bags of groceries in his arms.

"You're crazy," Barry said.

Donald ran three steps before he jumped. The unsecured rope flew in an arc behind him.

"See, it's easy!" Donald called from the other side. He set the grocery bags on the ice. Again he took a running start and leapt across the gap. His hood fell backward as he ran. Now he stood before them, smiling, his hair curling out from his cap.

"Coming?" he asked.

"You're crazy." Barry folded his arms across the leather jacket.

Donald looked at him quizzically. Suddenly he bent over and took the remaining groceries from the sled. He wedged Mary's briefcase between the bags.

Mary watched from the corner of her eye as he carried the bags across the water, the rope trailing after him. He set them down by the others.

When Donald jumped back, he didn't say anything.

Barry took a step backwards. "Come on, Mary."

Mary looked at him over her shoulder.

Donald picked up a sleeping bag. He tossed it over the gap.

"Ignore him," Barry said.

Donald threw the other sleeping bag across, then the knapsacks, one by one. Last of all he heaved the sled across. It landed with a clatter.

"I'm leaving!" Barry turned and began to walk away.

Donald was coiling the free end of the rope. When he finished he came toward Mary, holding out the end, ready to make it fast around her again.

Mary moved out of reach. She sensed that Barry had stopped and stood not far away, watching her.

Without thinking she ran forward. She threw her arms skyward as she jumped. Midway across the chasm, suspended in the darkening air, she realized where she was. But even then she had no sense of what she was doing or why she was doing it. She only knew that she was in motion, perilous motion, a chill wind full against her face. And now, beneath her, the ice was rising to meet her feet.

House Guest

A black Jaguar pulled into the driveway at half past six. Roy's armchair faced the bay window, and he looked up from his book when he heard the spray of gravel. He turned his head and called, "She's here!"

His wife ran down the stairs, buttoning her shirt as she came. She had been upstairs for more than an hour, opening and closing bureau drawers. Now as she walked around the baby, who sat on the carpet, she stepped on a rubber toy, making it squeal loudly.

"Quick, tell me the truth," she said, bending to pick up the toy. "Do I look all right?"

She wore a red shirt and a blue skirt with small yellow flowers on it. Her blond hair had been pulled into a knot, held by a silver clip, but loose strands fell around her neck and forehead. Makeup was streaked across her face, and it didn't hide the shadows under her eyes. She had been up since 5 A.M. cleaning the house and finishing new curtains for the spare room.

"You look beautiful," he said.

"Oh, go on," she said. "I didn't have a chance to tell you before, Roy, but thanks for clearing your things out of the guest room."

He smiled. Normally the spare room was his study. Now she called it the guest room. "It's only for one night, after all," he said. "And I know how much this visit means to you."

The woman coming to visit was his wife's oldest friend. They had met in kindergarten and had come up through high school together. Since those days they kept in touch with Christmas cards and the occasional telephone call. They hadn't seen each other for sixteen years.

"Like my hair this way?" his wife said, rubbing her hands on her skirt.

"It's fine," Roy said.

She shook her head slightly, and another strand of hair fell free of the clip. "I thought it looked more sophisticated," she said. "Lord, I'm nervous." She didn't have many friends. She tended to be awkward around new people, especially since the baby came.

"Maybe she's nervous, too," he said.

His wife stooped and picked up the baby. A scrap of material from the new curtains stuck to the baby's shirt, and she carefully plucked it off. The material was dark blue with white flecks, like a winter sky cluttered with stars.

"I like those new curtains," he said. "I'm looking forward to working in that room."

"You don't notice a thing when you're working," his wife said.

The front door swung open. A woman's voice said, "Joan!" She was tall, this woman, and lean, with glossy dark hair shaped to her head like a helmet. Her face was hidden by his wife's embrace.

The baby, sandwiched between them, began to cry. "It's okay," Roy told her. "They like each other."

The woman pulled back, keeping her hands on Joan's shoulders. "It's been a while," she said. Joan had tears in her eyes. "And what's all this?" the woman said, looking at the baby and then at Roy.

"Cecily, this is Roy," his wife said. "My husband. And the baby's name is Diane. After Roy's mother, we named her."

Roy extended his right hand. Cecily ignored him. She stared at the crying baby.

"How old is the little one?" she said.

"Just seven months," Joan said. "Born on the fifteenth of November."

Cecily had the biggest eyes Roy had ever seen. They were green, surrounded by spidery dark lashes.

"Isn't she something," Cecily said.

Diane cried louder. His wife rocked her, gently.

"I'll get her a bottle," Joan said. She handed the baby to Roy, who held her in both arms. "And something for us, too. You like gin and tonic, Cecily?"

"Do you have lime?" Cecily brushed a thread from her sleeve. Joan nodded. "That's fine, then," Cecily said. "I couldn't bear the taste of quinine without lime."

"Please, sit down," Roy said, as Joan went into the kitchen. He settled with the baby in the brown armchair. Cecily sat on the sofa and crossed her legs. She was wearing a knit dress with a wide black belt at its waist.

"So you're Roy," she said.

Roy didn't know what to say. He bounced the baby on his lap, until she stopped crying.

Cecily glanced at the baby. "She's different-looking," she said. "I can't see you in her at all. But then, you're not a bit as I pictured you."

"Is that so?" Roy said.

"From what Joan said, I expected you to be older," Cecily said.

Roy wondered what Joan had told this woman. "Older than what?" he said.

"Here we are, ready or not." Joan carried in a tray, on which glasses rattled precariously. But she set it on the table without spilling anything. She gave Roy Diane's bottle of formula. Then she handed Cecily a frosted glass. Roy set the baby, who now held her bottle, on the carpet and took a drink for himself.

His wife raised her glass. "To old friends," she said.

"And best friends," Cecily said. They all drank.

Roy turned to Cecily. "Joan says you're on your way to Canada. Is it business or pleasure?"

Cecily's eyes focused on his with such intensity that he wanted to look away. But he held her gaze. "Both," she said. Joan fluffed out her skirt and sat down next to Cecily on the sofa. "Cecily's expanding her design firm up north, Roy," she said. "I know I told you that."

Cecily smiled. "Several Canadian outfits have approached me," she said. She patted his wife's knee. "I promised Joan that the very next time I travelled north, I'd take a detour and look her up."

"I thought it would never ever happen," Joan said. "You spend so much time flitting from place to place, and travelling abroad." Her voice drawled the last word, managing to make it sound anything but exotic.

Over the years Cecily had sent them dozens of postcards. His wife kept them all, displayed on the fireplace mantle and the dining room bookshelves. They were pictures of Hong Kong, Geneva, Brussels, Johannesburg. On their backs raced Cecily's handwriting, narrow and spiky, impossible for Roy to read—although Joan claimed it gave her no difficulty.

"I'm making New York my home," Cecily was saying. "I bought a condominium overlooking the East River. And there's a swimming pool, where I swim in the evenings. You'll have to visit." She patted Joan's knee again, then stretched her long fingers toward Roy. "Both of you must come," she said.

Roy did not like New York. To him the city meant dirt and noise and bad manners, to say nothing of the social inequities. But his wife's eyes were shining. "We would love to do that," she said. "We're pretty much out of touch with things here."

"Let me get refills," Roy said. He carefully moved the baby away from his feet. She lay back on the carpet and watched him collect the others' glasses. "Diane's sleepy," he said.

"I'll be taking her up to bed in a minute," Joan said.

As he mixed drinks in the kitchen, Roy heard Cecily's voice, low and rhythmic, in the next room. He thought how different the two women were. From her glossy fingernails to her high-heeled shoes, the details of Cecily's appearance had a precision to them, as if they had been planned far in advance. And her movements were poised, mannered. Instead of blinking, she periodically lowered her eyelids, slowly, and slowly opened them again. Her eyelids were elongated and powdered a pale shade of green.

Joan, on the other hand, moved and dressed as if in a state of constant fluster. Her fingernails were ragged, her hair generally was in disarray. Her voice wavered and she couldn't tell an anecdote—she never remembered the beginning of a story by the time she'd reached its end, and even the names of the characters would change. His sweet, warmhearted, awkward wife!

In the living room, Cecily had stopped talking. He picked up the tray of drinks and marched toward the door.

Then he heard both women break into laughter. Roy stood by the kitchen door, not wanting to interrupt them. For a moment they seemed to be whispering. Now, they began to laugh again. Roy watched bits of ice float in the glasses as he stood there, listening to the unexpectedly guttural sound of their laughter. He had a sudden desire to put down the tray and walk away from them—walk right out of the house.

*   *   *

But the feeling passed once he came into the living room. The women smiled at him and said thank-you for their drinks.

When Joan carried the baby upstairs to bed, Cecily followed them with her eyes. "Isn't she something," she said.

"Ever tempted to have one of your own?" Roy said.

Cecily tapped her fingernails against her glass. "Maybe I never met the right father," she said.

"Maybe you will," he said quickly. "That is, if you want to. It's an odd business." Then he thought, what in hell do I mean by that?

"Maybe." Cecily smiled. "Tell me about your work. From what Joan said, all I understood was something about a phonetic dictionary?"

"Not quite," he said. "We're analyzing regional variations in speech."

"I'm amazed that any are left," she said. "We live in such a homogenized culture. What constitutes a variation?"

Normally he didn't talk about the project. But this woman seemed genuinely interested. "We're looking at the derivations of pronunciation differences," he said. "A variation, or what we call a regionalism, refers to pronunciation habits common to a particular area." As he went on, she asked intelligent questions. Before he realized it, he had traced the entire procedure—from recording a dialect, to making a pho-

netic transcript, comparing it to others, analyzing the variations, and speculating on their evolution.

"You must be so sensitive to sounds," she said, her eyes
bright. "When you hear a voice, you must hear things that the
rest of us miss entirely."

"Not really," he said. "I hear what you hear. I'm more ex-
perienced in identifying various inflections and word choices,
that's all." He took a long sip of his drink.

"When I speak, do you hear Iowa or New York?" she asked.

"Your speech is curiously free of the regional inflections I
would expect. My guess would be that you've studied with a
voice coach."

"Hardly." Cecily's eyes narrowed. "What makes you think
so?"

"Well, it's unusual not to retain at least a trace of the speech
patterns prevalent in one's hometown," he said. "You grew up
with Joan, yet hers are flat, typically Central Midland, while
yours sound broad, almost British."

"In other words, I sound like a real hick," his wife said, from
the foot of the stairs.

"Not at all," he said, surprised. He hadn't heard her come
down.

"Dinner's just about ready," she said. "Maybe you'd like to
take a look at your room, Cecily?"

"Marvelous." Cecily stood up. "I left my overnight bag in
the car."

"I'll get that," Roy said.

As the women went upstairs, he heard Cecily say, "Tell me,
Joan. Did you put on a great deal of weight in your pregnancy?"

Roy found the suitcase in the back seat of the car, which
smelled strongly of Cecily's perfume. He grabbed the case
and pulled it out of the car.

The women were standing at the doorway of the spare
room, looking at it critically. Cecily said, "It's a wonderful
old house. Pure Victoriana. You were lucky to find it. All it
needs, really, is a good cleaning. And some decent curtains."

Roy put his hand on his wife's shoulder. She turned away.

"I better check on dinner," she said, moving toward the stairs. Roy set Cecily's suitcase by the bureau.

"I meant what I said," Cecily told him, lowering her eyelids. "It's a wonderful house."

"Thanks," he said. "I'll let you get settled." Then he quickly followed his wife downstairs.

His wife was slamming down a pot lid in the kitchen. She didn't look up. He sat on a stool by the counter, which was covered with bowls and cutting boards and knives. The walls were hung with framed cross-stitched panels of fruits and vegetables that Joan had embroidered while she was pregnant.

After a while, Joan turned to him, a wooden spoon in her hand. "Can you tell me why we put ourselves through this?" she said. "Why do we invite strangers into our home?"

"Not so long ago you said she was your best friend." Roy smiled and slid off the stool. "Try to relax a little," he said, moving to hug her.

But Joan stepped aside. She threw open the oven door. "That woman is pure poison," she said, reaching inside.

* * *

At dinner Cecily praised his wife's cooking. "I haven't had pot roast like this in years," she said.

Joan didn't say much. She served the vegetables while Roy carved the roast. Then she refilled the wineglasses. Her fork pushed food around her plate, and she stared at the wallpaper as if she had never seen it before.

"I suppose you don't have much time to cook, in New York," Roy said to Cecily.

"No, I eat on the run," Cecily said. She cut a tiny sliver of meat. "Once a week the woman who cleans my place does me a casserole, and I nibble at that when I'm in."

"You have a cleaning woman?" The wine had flushed Joan's cheeks and made her Midland accent more pronounced.

Cecily chewed the meat with a small, rapid motion that made the edges of her lips quiver. "I couldn't live without my daily," she said. "Don't you have a woman come in?"

"Now you must be joking," his wife said.

"Oh, darling," Cecily said, "how can you cope? Between the house and the baby, how do you find time to keep yourself together?" She added, "Not to mention Roy."

Joan turned her chair to face Cecily. "People like us can't afford a maid," she said. "You don't know what it's like."

"You left your job, didn't you, dear, when the baby came," Cecily said. She shook her head. "Babies can be tyrants."

Roy set his fork on his plate. "Joan does free-lance work," he said. His wife stared at the tablecloth. "And she's active in the University Women's Club."

"I went to one meeting," Joan said. "One. And believe me, that was the last one." She poured herself another glass of wine. "They asked me don't you play bridge? You don't play bridge? Well then, there's our book club." Joan mimicked the voices, anglicizing the nouns. "Know what kind of book club they had? They read *French.*"

Roy hadn't heard this story before. He took the wine bottle when she set it down. "More wine, Cecily?" he said.

"I couldn't possibly," Cecily said. She pressed her narrow fingers against the base of her throat, in a delicate gesture.

"Shall we adjourn to the living room?" Roy said.

"French," Joan repeated.

Cecily pushed back her chair. "I'll be back in a flash," she said.

Joan watched her leave the room. "Don't rush," she said, her voice low.

"Take it easy," Roy said.

Joan's eyes, brown and slightly bloodshot, focused on him. "More wine, Cecily?" she said in a deep, flat voice imitating Roy's. "Oh no, I couldn't possibly," she said, her voice high-pitched and exaggeratedly precise. She made a sweeping gesture with one arm, upsetting the wine bottle.

Roy righted the bottle before any wine spilled. "Come on," he said to her. "I'll help you clear up."

Joan stood up, bracing herself with both hands on the table. "For such a highly educated person, Roy, you don't know a whole lot," she said.

Roy looked at her. Her skirt was creased, and a brown stain

marked the front of her shirt. Her hair, almost entirely free of its clip now, hung limply around her face. "Why can't you pull yourself together?" he said.

Her mouth fell open, like that of a child hurt too unexpectedly to cry. He felt ashamed of himself. But before he could say anything she swept past him and went into the kitchen.

Roy cleared the table. He carried the plates to the kitchen, where he scraped and stacked them. Joan sat in a chair by the counter, turned away from him. He went back to the dining room to collect the glasses. He was holding the wineglasses when he heard the noises. Directly overhead, the floorboards were creaking in the room above. Someone was in their bedroom.

He listened to footsteps move from one side of the room to the other. Cecily. What could she be up to in there?

He thought of telling Joan. He thought of going upstairs himself. But what could either of them say? The woman was a guest in their home.

The footsteps stopped. He tried to fix their position in the room. "Hell," he said. He took the stairs two at a time, the wineglasses still in his hand.

When he entered the bedroom, Cecily was standing in the corner by the closet, facing him, as if she were waiting for him. He stood just inside the doorway, suddenly feeling ill at ease. She smiled. She never took her eyes off him as she moved across the room.

He clutched the glasses. When she reached him she put up her hands and lightly held his head between them. Then she leaned forward and kissed him.

Her lips were moist. He closed his eyes. When he opened them, she glided away.

He listened to the sound of her high-heeled shoes as they moved off, down the hallway, toward the guest room.

*   *   *

Roy sat in his armchair, balancing a brandy snifter on his knee. His wife sat in her rocking chair, drinking another glass of wine. He had never seen her drink so much before.

"Hitting that stuff pretty hard, aren't you?" he said.

She lifted her glass, as if toasting him. "Even the hired hands get a drink at the end of the day," she said.

When Cecily came down, she sat in the middle of the sofa.

"Did you find what you were looking for?" Roy said.

Cecily held up a leather-bound book. Then she patted the cushions on either side of her. "You'll have to sit here to appreciate this," she said.

Roy moved first. His wife watched him, then stood up. "Why not," she said. She sat on Cecily's left.

"Recognize this?" Cecily asked her.

Joan set her wine on the coffee table. "It's the *Echo,*" she said. "Lord. I haven't looked at that for years. I'm not sure I even have my copy anymore."

Cecily turned to Roy. "Our high school yearbook," she said. Roy sensed the shape of her leg, beneath the knit dress, close beside him. Her perfume filled his head. He began to shift away. But Cecily opened the book so that its right-hand page lay across his thigh.

"That's the front door," his wife said, looking down at a photograph of a brick building with narrow windows. "Down there is the gully."

"We went there when we skipped classes," Cecily said.

"That's where we smoked cigarettes," Joan said. She smiled.

"But some of us smoked other stuff, right?" Cecily said. Joan laughed.

Roy cleared his throat. He had never known that his wife smoked cigarettes, let alone anything else.

Cecily turned the page. "That's Dr. Evans, the principal," she said. "He made a deal with Joan. If she stopped forging passes, he said, he would cancel half of her detention time."

"Detention time?" Roy said.

"That was the penalty for fighting or cutting classes," Joan said. "That old geezer!"

Cecily flicked through the pages. "Here we are," she said. "The class photo. Can you spot us, Roy?"

He scanned the photograph. A group of adolescents stood

in tiers. Their clothes and hairstyles seemed ornate, anti-quated. "They all look alike," he said.

"Here." Cecily's red fingernail traced a circle around two heads. He stared down into the faces of nearly identical girls. "You look like twins!" he said.

Both girls in the picture were smiling, and both wore white sweaters. Their hair was long and dark, parted in the middle and curled at the ends.

Roy looked up from the photograph, across Cecily's knees, to stare at his wife. He had known that she dyed her hair, of course. But except for her baby pictures, he had never seen her as a brunette.

"I remember when they took that picture," his wife said. "Mrs. Burgess dragged me to the girls' room and scrubbed off all my makeup before the photographer came. That old bitch!"

Cecily turned the page. She said. "Remember Mike Adams, Joan?"

"God, could he kiss," his wife said.

Cecily flipped the page. "There you are!" Joan said.

Roy had to read the name to be sure the picture was of Cecily, not his wife. Joan read its caption: "Favorite color, red. Favorite song, 'Money Can't Buy Me Love.' Voted Most Likely to Succeed."

Roy glanced at his wife. "What were you voted?"

"They voted me Class Clown!" She and Cecily broke into gales of laughter. Roy watched them as they laughed, their heads tipped back, their mouths open wide.

Upstairs, the baby began to scream.

"I'll go!" He jumped up from the sofa. "I'll take care of her," he said. "Then I think I'll turn in myself."

"We'll be up in a while," his wife said.

"We've got some catching up to do," Cecily said. "Sweet dreams."

He felt her eyes on him all the way up the stairs.

The baby seemed to have fallen asleep again. He listened outside her door for a moment. Then he went to the bedroom. His typewriter and papers lay on top of his bureau. He had moved them there from the spare room that morning. They appeared untouched.

Nothing in the room seemed disturbed. He undressed and got into bed, leaving the bedside lamp on for his wife. He stared at the ceiling, listening hard for some noise from downstairs. All he heard was the bathroom tap dripping water. By imagining the water in slow motion—shivering, ovoid globules that broke with a splat when each hit the porcelain sink—he managed at last to drift into sleep.

*   *   *

He awoke with a start. Down the hall, the baby was crying. Beside him, the place where his wife always slept was empty.

Roy didn't bother to put on his slippers or robe. Wearing only pajama bottoms, he ran down the hall.

The nursery was lit by a night-light shaped like a duck. He bent over the crib. The baby's face was red from crying. Her arms and legs were drawn up, and her hands were clenched. He picked her up and cradled her in his arms.

"Shhh, Diane. It's okay," he whispered. "You had a bad dream."

He tried to give her the bottle of formula on her dressing table. But she turned her face away and cried harder. She kept crying while he changed her diaper. Then he carried her back and forth across the nursery, trying to soothe her. Eventually, her crying slowed. At last it stopped. The baby sighed, then yawned. He looked at her small red face, wondering what she felt. Her hands gradually unclenched, and her legs grew limp. At last her eyes closed. He paused near the night-light, trying to gauge the depth of her sleep.

When he had settled the baby into her crib, and covered her with a blanket, he felt proud of himself. Normally Joan handled things if the baby woke in the night.

As he stepped into the hallway, he thought he heard someone whispering. The sound intensified, then wavered into silence. The door to the guest room stood half-open. Yellow light spilled into the hallway from a dim lamp inside. He walked by the room in a rush, his eyes straight ahead. He thought he heard them laughing as he passed.

The next morning he awoke late, feeling groggy. His wife's side of the bed remained empty.

As he came down the stairs, he heard the women laughing. For a moment he felt like going back to bed. Then he reminded himself that, after all, Cecily would be leaving soon. Later this morning he could move his typewriter back to the spare room and get down to work.

Roy made himself enter the dining room. His wife was at the table, opening a jar of her homemade raspberry jam. She looked oddly formal to him. Then he realized that her hairstyle was different—sleeker, pulled back behind her ears—and that she was wearing a suit.

Cecily sat at the table's head, nibbling at a slice of toast. She waved her fingers at him.

The baby cooed from her high chair.

"You slept late." His wife dipped a knife into the jam.

"I saved you a piece of toast," Cecily said.

He poured himself a cup of coffee. "I was up in the night with the baby," he said. He added milk and stirred the coffee.

Cecily smiled.

"You can take the night watch tonight," he said, turning to his wife.

Joan glanced at Cecily.

"Roy," Cecily said. "I have a proposition for you."

He looked hard at her.

"I've invited Joan to come along to Canada with me," Cecily said.

Roy stared at his wife. "I would love to go," Joan said quickly.

"Joan hasn't had a minute to herself since Diane was born," Cecily said. "She can come with me and share my hotel accommodations."

"I could go shopping," Joan said. "Sightseeing. Things like that."

"It will give us a chance to get reacquainted," Cecily said.

"It's a chance we might never ever have again," Joan said.

He listened, looking from one to the other.

"Think of all the work you can do, with me out of the house," his wife said.

"But the baby," he said.

"Diane's easy. She sleeps most of the time," she said.

"It *is* summer vacation," Cecily said. "Joan told me you had no plans to get away."

Roy found he was still stirring his coffee. He placed the spoon in the saucer. "I don't know what I can say," he said to his wife. "It sounds as if you already decided."

"All right!" Joan said. "I told you he'd go along with it," she said, looking at Cecily.

Cecily's eyes never left Roy. "She already packed her bag," she said softly.

Then Cecily began to talk about patterns in china and flatware. His wife listened raptly. Roy finished his coffee.

"It's time!" Cecily said.

Roy carried the suitcases out to the car. Joan followed, holding the baby and giving her one last hug. As Roy slid the cases into the trunk, Cecily appeared, carrying a jar of home-made jam and her copy of the *Echo.*

Roy slammed down the lid of the car's trunk. "You know Diane's schedule as well as I do," Joan said. "Just remember, alternate the apple juice with the formula."

She handed the baby to Cecily. Then she put her arms around Roy and squeezed his shoulders.

"I'm not sure it's a good idea, you leaving like this," he said. "You can manage just fine," Joan said. "Diane's no trouble. You did fine last night. Besides, it's only for a couple of days."

"A week at the most," Cecily said.

The baby wrapped her hand around Cecily's forefinger. Cecily suddenly shook her finger free. "Christ," she said. "Why don't you cut its nails." She thrust the baby into Roy's arms.

The women slid into the car's front seat. They smiled at Roy through the open window, their faces glossy with makeup. They both wore tailored suits, and they looked like sisters. Their eyes were full of secrets.

Cecily started the motor and flicked on the car's air conditioner. She pressed a button on the wood-panelled dashboard, and the car window hissed shut.

"Good-bye," Roy said.

He held the baby against his shoulder as the Jaguar backed out of the driveway. Just before it pulled away, Joan turned to look at him through the closed window. She opened her mouth, as if to tell him something. But he couldn't hear her.

"What are you saying, Joan?" he said. Then something in him snapped. "I can't understand you!" he shouted. "Go to hell for all I care!"

She smiled and nodded. The baby clung to his shirt with both hands as the car swept down the street, rounded a corner, and disappeared.

Smoke

He called her from Connecticut and said he had left his wife.

The moment she recognized his voice, she began to dance. She moved in an erratic fox-trot, a step she hadn't used since boarding school, from end to end of the narrow kitchen. Her reflection glimmered in the black glass of the wall oven. She was a small, dark-haired woman, but her reflection burst with light.

She said to herself, be careful.

"I finished moving today," he said. Behind his voice cars honked and a siren wailed. He must be using a pay phone on the street, she thought. She pictured him wearing his old leather jacket, its collar turned up against his chin.

"I found a place along the shore," he said. "It reminds me of the cottage you had."

She stopped dancing. Steam curled away from the TV dinner waiting on the formica-topped table. She looked down at her hand, still wearing an oven-proof mitt.

"I miss you," he said.

She slid off the mitt and examined her fingernails, which looked narrow and frail. "Do you?" she said.

"You should come here," he said. "Come for the weekend."

She cleared her throat. "Let me think about it," she said.

"Alice?" His voice sounded deep and rough. His "at home" voice she had called it, scoffing at the other, polished voice he used to fend off outsiders.

"I need to think about it," she said. "I'll call you."

"You can't call me," he said, his voice full of regret. "I don't know my new telephone number."

"You haven't changed, Dennis," she said. He had never remembered telephone numbers or calendar dates. Or numbers of any kind.

"You're wrong," he said. "I'm a new man. I'm living by the ocean now. I have a place like the one you had."

She thought of the living room at her old cottage. She saw herself standing on a chair to reach the top of a window, stretching lengths of masking tape across it to form an X, while Dennis watched her from the sofa.

The precautions proved not to be necessary. The hurricane had veered off course, missing Connecticut altogether. But she and Dennis sat out the warning period, drinking beer and playing old Beatles records on the stereo. It was the only time they spent an entire night together.

"Alice? Will you come?"

"I don't know," she said.

"I'll meet your train," he said. "Friday after work?"

"This Friday?" She had promised to have dinner with James, an administrator at the museum where she worked. He was a quiet, unassuming man. She liked that. Quiet and safe.

"I need you, Alice." Dennis said it slowly, as if quoting a popular song.

"Damn," she said. Her fingers played with the telephone cord.

"I'll meet your train." The siren in the background grew louder.

"But I don't know the train times," she said.

"I'll meet all the trains." A sing-song voice cut in behind his, asking him to deposit another coin. She heard him shout "Alice" and "Friday" and another word that she couldn't make out. Then the line went dead.

Slowly, she replaced the receiver. With her other hand she rubbed her ear. She sat at the table and watched the last threads of steam escape from her dinner.

Later, as she was going to bed, she thought, he never asked about me. A year is a long time. Anything might have happened.

*   *   *

After work on Friday, she went to the station, wearing a new coat made of soft blue wool. She had broken her date with James, saying only that a friend needed her.

It was her favorite time of day in New York. Sunlight slanted into the streets, turning them faintly golden. From the train window she watched the city recede, the light playing along the red and grey and light brown stones of the buildings.

At the station newsstand she had pulled a book from the shelf and paid for it hurriedly. The book, she saw now, was an Iris Murdoch novel that she had read years ago, when she was at Yale. She began to read, but stopped after only three pages. The characters and the plot seemed gratuitously complicated. Yet once she had liked that sort of thing.

Everything was dark by the time the train reached New Haven. The car smelled of cigarettes and liquor from the commuters. She took a deep breath as she stepped down from the train. The station smelled of stale air and soot.

Dennis stood in the center of the platform, his hands in his overcoat pockets, his head and shoulders curved forward. When he saw her, he straightened and threw his cigarette onto the tracks.

He was a big man, well over six feet tall. He took long strides to reach her. Once she had stood still on a street corner in Manhattan, unable to move after seeing a stranger walk as Dennis did.

He came up to her and put his hand on her shoulder without speaking. When he pressed his cheek against hers, his face felt cold and rough—very like the face of a cousin who had embraced her with unexpected passion at her mother's funeral.

She pulled back to see him. His eyes were bloodshot. His dark red hair wanted cutting, and his shirt needed ironing. But his features were as finely drawn as ever, and the intelligence in his eyes made her take a step away from him. "You've grown taller, if that's possible," she said. His face, dark with freckles, looked full, as if he had put on weight.

"You're just the same," he said. She had lost ten pounds and grown her hair long. "It's been a long time," he said, smiling.

"One year," she said. When he smiled, he seemed like a stranger.

He took her hand as they walked down the platform. He wore expensive-looking leather gloves, and she thought that they must be new. Otherwise, he would have lost one, or burnt cigarette holes in them.

She wondered if the gloves were a gift from Shelley, his wife.

"The car's over here," he said. His voice sounded hoarse, as if he had a cold.

She glanced around the parking lot, half expecting to see someone that she knew.

Then she saw the car. "No more Volkswagen?" she said. She recognized the green BMW. Shelley had bought it new, two years ago.

"Shelley's selling it to me," he said.

He hadn't locked the car doors. She smoothed her coat beneath her as she sat down. The back seat and floor were covered with things: paperback books, newspapers, two pairs of tennis shoes, candy wrappers, soda cans, an empty scotch bottle, a corduroy jacket, a carton of cigarettes, three or four striped shirts, two bright-pink parking tickets, and a pile of record albums (with *Aretha Franklin Live in Paris* and *The Best of the Temptations* visible on top).

They drove. He didn't say anything. In the old days they never had enough time to talk. This silence seemed embarrassing. She watched the traffic lights and read the street names, willing the city to seem familiar again.

Suddenly he pulled the car into a parking lot. "Where are we going?" Alice said.

"I thought we would have a drink."

Before she could respond, he climbed out of the car. She hurried to catch up.

He walked without looking back at her. The bar was two flights down from the street, in an old, brick-lined cellar. Blue-tinted mirrors lined the walls. Men and women in business suits sat at the bar and at small, round tables, talking and smoking and drinking.

"Hi, Denny," a waitress said, tipping a round empty tray against her left hip. She sat them at a table in the corner and left without saying more, as if she knew what they would order.

"I remember this place," Alice said, looking at the mirror above their table. "This is the place where you proposed to me."

The waitress set down a bucket of ice by their table. "Back in a sec," she said.

"You asked me to marry you," Alice said. "And I said, 'But Dennis, you're already married.'"

"Just leave it, Paula," Dennis said to the waitress. She put a bottle of champagne on the table before him, then hesitated. "I remembered," the waitress said.

"That's great," Dennis told her.

The waitress took the bottle again. She had trouble removing the cork. "My wrist must be too small," she said.

Dennis stretched out his hand for the bottle. He opened the champagne without fanfare. The waitress went away, looking disappointed. Alice thought of the old days, when he would shake the bottle to send the cork flying across the room. He seemed to be always celebrating, then.

"You sang Beethoven's 'Ode to Joy,'" she said. She wished she could stop talking.

Dennis filled their glasses. "Did I?"

"We were sitting at that table near the bar. You don't remember that? You sang it in German, and when you finished, the people at the corner table cheered."

He lit a cigarette.

"I'm sorry. I'm talking too much," she said. "How's Shelley?"

He sighed. "Shelley's all right, Alice," he said. "What do you want me to tell you?"

"She hasn't killed herself, then? I thought that was the idea—that if you left, she did herself in."

He exhaled a long spiral of smoke. "I suppose I have this coming," he said.

She shook her head. "I'm sorry," she said again.

He raised his glass. "To you," he said.

Alice lifted her glass slowly. "Confusion to our enemies," she said.

As they drank Alice sensed someone staring at them. She

glanced around the room. But it was only a small boy, sitting at the bar next to his mother. He watched them in the wall mirror, staring over the rim of his glass of milk.

Alice looked away. "How are you, Dennis?" she said.

He looked straight into her eyes. "Okay."

"Work going well?"

He reached for the bottle and refilled their glasses. "I'm up for tenure," he said. He lit another cigarette.

"And are you likely to get it?"

"No," he said. "Not likely."

"Why not?"

He pulled a box of matches from his trouser pocket. "My politics aren't what they would like, of course," he said. He tapped the box against the table. "And, with one thing and another, I haven't been able to do much work lately."

He stubbed out the half-smoked cigarette. "Drink up," he said. As he reached for his glass, his hand shook. "It's nothing but smoke and mirrors anyway," he said.

"I'm sorry," she said. She took the red paper napkin from beneath her drink and twisted it between her hands.

"Don't ever be sorry for me, Alice," he said. "Come on, drink your champagne."

"It must be hard to write when you're teaching," she said.

He drummed his fingers on the table. "Shelley said I had a failure of vision." He grinned. He picked up the matchbox again, shaking it as if he liked the rattle of the wooden sticks inside. "I'd be lying if I said it was a happy time," he said.

Alice wanted to touch his shoulder. Instead, she folded her hands on the table. She made herself think of the time he had promised to feed her cat while she was out of town. He never came by, and the cat went half-crazy, using houseplants for a litter box, shredding curtains, and tearing holes in the sofa cushions.

She thought of the night he had called and asked her to meet him at a restaurant across town. She had waited for him for two hours. He never arrived.

But when he did meet her—usually after some university function so that he didn't have to invent an excuse for his wife—he was handsome, wearing a crumpled tie and dinner jacket that smelled of smoke from other men's pipes, and he was charming. He recited the first and last paragraphs of her favorite novels, he sang the blues, he took her dancing at roadhouses, he even took her to church—late at night, when nobody else was there. He emptied his pockets for street people, and he stopped to help motorists stranded on the interstate. And she knew he would do anything for her, if only he were free.

"Look," he said now. "We're being watched."

The boy at the bar set down his glass, keeping his eyes on their reflection. His eyes looked round and shiny as marbles. His mother talked to the bartender, her arm resting on the briefcase in her lap.

The waitress came to pour more champagne. "Everything okay here?" she said.

"Sure," Dennis said. "Just one thing before you bring the check. We want to stand the kid another round."

"The kid?" The waitress looked where Dennis pointed. The little boy stared back at them.

"We admire his manners," Dennis said. "Also his tailor."

"I'll tell him," the waitress said. She headed for the bar.

Dennis smiled at Alice. But she didn't smile back.

"You're so damned wonderful, aren't you?" she said suddenly.

The waitress returned with Dennis's credit card. "You've got yourself a fan," she said to him.

The boy had swivelled on the bar stool to look directly at them. A full glass of milk stood behind him on the bar.

"I could use a fan," Dennis said. He rested his hand on Alice's hands, still folded on the table. She pulled one hand free to rub her eyes.

Dennis drained his glass. "You'll like my new place," he said. "Come on. Let's get out of here."

As they walked to the door, the boy's mother hailed them. "Zachary's been watching you," she called from the bar. "He said he decided that he likes you both very much."

All the customers seemed to be watching them now, look-

ing on with approval. Dennis smiled. The little boy looked
away. Alice stood, half-hidden behind him, her arms limp at
her sides. She thought, no, I will not be charmed again.

*   *   *

As soon as he started the car, Dennis switched on the radio.
Classical music poured out. He quickly switched stations.

They were on the turnpike before he found music that he
liked—a station playing "Nowhere to Run, Nowhere to Hide"
by Gladys Knight and the Pips. Dennis sang along.

He sounded the car horn at appropriate places in the
music. Alice looked at him. "I'm happy," he said. He smiled
at her so sweetly that she smiled back.

They stopped twice—once at a liquor store, once at a truck
to buy lobsters. After each stop Dennis tossed a paper bag
into the back seat. The lobsters made feeble scuttling sounds.

"See, I remember some things," he said, starting the car
again.

Now she was confused. "Such as?"

"You forgot!" he said, his voice jubilant. "You don't remember our first date."

She remembered it clearly. They had met at a university
reception for a visiting lecturer. Alice overheard someone
make an irreverent remark about the lecture and she smiled.
Whereupon Dennis, who had made the remark, introduced
himself as the only other person present who possessed a
sense of humor. They fell into conversation easily, going on
from the reception to a pizza parlor. Dennis told the waitress
that they were celebrating Alice's birthday, and the pizza
came with a lit candle stuck in its center.

"You forgot, admit it," he said now.

"I don't see the connection," she said. Did he mean their
second date? That night they saw an Ingmar Bergman film.
Afterward he sat on the back porch at her cottage and told
her, "The love has gone out of my marriage." Lobster had not
been mentioned.

"Time's up!" he said. He leaned across and kissed her,
keeping one hand on the steering wheel. "On our first date
we ate lobsters at the Chart House."

"Oh," she said. She had been inside the Chart House only once, for brunch with a group of graduate students.

He stopped at a traffic light. "She forgot our first date," he said, shaking his head and smiling.

She crossed her arms. Who had he taken to the Chart House?

*   *   *

The driveway ended at a modern, wood-shingled house. A light burned over the front door. "We'll have the place all to ourselves tonight," he said.

"Don't you always?"

"I share it," he said. "I thought I told you."

He reached into the back seat for the bags. Alice pulled out her oversized shoulder bag.

Outside a strong wind blew, smelling of the sea.

"Long Island Sound is our backyard," he said, as he unlocked the house's front door. "I'll show you tomorrow."

"Tomorrow?" she said. "I'm going back tonight."

He opened the door, seeming not to hear her.

She followed him inside, through a living room with a high ceiling and a fireplace, into an enormous kitchen. He set the paper bags on a gleaming tiled counter. "My roommates are architects. Neal and Rawlings. Heard of them?"

She shook her head.

He took a bottle of white wine out of a bag. "Cowboy architects," he said.

"Cowboy architects?"

"You'll meet them tomorrow. You'll see." He searched through a drawer. "They wear funny boots and Stetsons."

"Both of them?"

His hand came out of the drawer holding a corkscrew. "Neal and Rawlings," he said. "My roomies." He opened the bottle.

In a cupboard he found two water tumblers. He filled them with wine and handed one to Alice. "Confusion to our enemies," he said.

The wine was warm. She followed him into the living room. He set down his glass and bent over an elaborate stereo system. "Last time I almost broke it," he said.

She sat on a leather sofa in front of the fireplace. He put on an Otis Redding record.

He sat next to her, but almost at once he stood up again. "What I'd like to do, if you don't object, is have a quick shower," he said.

"Go ahead," she said, surprised.

He bounded up the stairs, the glass of wine in his hand.

The leather sofa felt cold. After listening to the record for a while, she began to shiver. She stood up, rubbing her arms. A box of split wood and kindling lay next to the fireplace, and she thought, why not.

The last fire she had built was at Girl Scout camp, but the pile of wood and kindling she assembled looked authentic. She found matches on the mantle, next to an autographed photo of Dolly Parton.

As the fire caught, she felt more cheerful. She carefully set the fire screen in place and went out to the kitchen to pour herself more wine.

Glass in hand, she paused to read the bulletin board by the telephone. A small confederate flag was pinned up next to a wedge of stapled telephone bills with some numbers circled in red. A newspaper clipping about I. M. Pei had an obscenity scrawled over its headline. Near the bottom of the board a pencilled note read: "Neal. Call Melinda. She say Fri. no go." Underneath, in different handwriting, were the words: "Okay if Friday's mine? Dennis."

Dennis's voice said, "Alice!"

She looked toward the living room. It was full of smoke. Dennis, a towel wrapped around his waist, was trying to force open a window. She ran to the front door and opened it wide.

Coughing, Dennis gave up on the window. He used a poker to break up the fire. Alice ran back to the kitchen. She took a saucepan from a wall rack, filled it with water, then carried it quickly back to the fireplace. The water doused the remaining flames with a hiss. Smoke moved toward the door slowly, in long coils.

Dennis stood by the door, hands on his hips. Streaks of soot across his face made him seem younger. Unexpectedly she felt a surge of affection for him. She walked to his side.

"Don't you know anything about flues?" he said. "For God's sake!"

He had never spoken roughly to her before. Now that the fire was out, she had expected him to be amused.

"This place smells like an incinerator," he said. "What am I going to do?"

"It isn't so bad now," she said. "I'm sorry." She felt more than sorry; she was appalled by her own carelessness.

"I only moved in here last week," he said. "They'll think I'm an idiot."

"They'll forgive you," she said. "After all, it wasn't your fault. I'll explain."

Dennis pushed his hair back from his eyes, leaving more soot on his forehead.

"Look," she said. "Do you have any spray? Room deodorizer. You know, the stuff they advertise on television." She thought with grim irony of the commercials showing women afraid of smells in their homes.

"I don't know," he said. "Do they work?"

"Of course," she said. She had never used any.

Neither, it seemed, had the cowboy architects. After searching the cupboards, Dennis drove to a Kwik-Stop Market, next to the local gas station. Alice went in and came out with two aerosol cans of deodorizer.

When they got back, Alice went from room to room, sweeping the air with the spray. Upstairs, she sprayed two large bedrooms, but left the third alone. Dennis's room, that was. Over the bed hung a painting she remembered from the apartment he had shared with Shelley, an Impressionist treatment of a man sleeping on a park bench. Alice was touched by the sight of the single bed with its plaid bedspread. She had seen the satin-covered king-sized bed in his old apartment only once, but the thought of it haunted her.

When she came downstairs, Dennis was slumped in a chair, smoking a cigarette by the open window. "Better?" she said.

"It smells like a hospital," he said. "A smoky hospital."

Shivering, she looked around for her coat. Dennis threw his cigarette out the window. "Come on," he said. "Let's get something to eat." He stood up.

"What about the lobsters?" she said.

"They seem to be dead," he said. "I checked while you were spraying."

"Probably asphyxiated," she said. He didn't laugh. She saw her coat then, crushed on the chair where he had been sitting, a streak of soot across its sleeve.

They had dinner at an Italian restaurant nearby. Alice found the red checked tablecloths curiously comforting. Dennis ordered a vodka and tonic, and he didn't speak until his glass was empty. Then he said, "I shouted at you back there."

"That's okay," she said. "I deserved it."

He shook his head. "It was myself I was mad at," he said. "I wanted to make a fresh start. But I always screw things up."

The waitress came for the third time to take their order. They decided to share a pizza.

"Can you see if they'll put a candle on it?" Dennis asked the waitress. "It's my wife's birthday."

                    *   *   *

Afterward, during the drive back to the house, Alice's face still felt hot with embarrassment. The sparkler stuck in the pizza had been bad enough. But when the waitress served them complimentary spumoni and sang "Happy Birthday," she had wanted to disappear.

Dennis nodded his head in time to imaginary music.

Alice looked out at the flat roadside. Here and there she saw blackness that must be the sea.

Dennis began to sing. "I. Been. Loving you. Too long," he sang, "to stop now."

"Otis Redding," Alice said. "Music to start fires by."

He reached over and patted her knee. The sight of his leather glove against the thin fabric of her dress made her nervous.

"Did you see my room when you were upstairs?" he said suddenly.

"I think so," she said.

"It's the small one. Looks like something out of Ozzie and Harriet."

"Yes," she said. "Very Spartan. Not in keeping with your roommates' general decor."

"They didn't decorate it," he said. "They're renters, same as I am." He stopped the car in the driveway. "I thought we would sleep in Neal's room tonight," he said.

Alice's stomach clenched. "Won't Neal mind?" she said faintly.

Dennis looked over at her, his eyes barely visible in the light that came from the house. "You're nervous?" he said.

"I planned to go home," she said. "All of this seems to be happening rather fast."

"That's the last thing I would expect you to say," he said. "It's been more than a year."

She rested her hand on the door handle. The touch of the cold chrome steadied her. "How is Shelley?" she said.

Dennis yawned. "Shelley is Shelley," he said. "She goes around with an accountant now. An accountant." He yawned again. "I'm sorry, Alice. I know I'm not the best company just now."

She tried to think of words to reassure him. They went inside without speaking.

A thin haze hung over the living room. "I guess it was worse than I thought," Alice said.

"Maybe it's better upstairs." He went up the stairs ahead of her. She took her time, pausing to look back at the dark living room.

"Come and see this," Dennis called.

He switched on a light in one of the bedrooms. The light bulb was red. A twelve-foot Confederate flag was pinned to the ceiling over the bed. The room was strewn with men's clothing. It smelled of smoke and Lysol.

Alice thought, hell might be like this room.

*   *   *

She woke suddenly. The red light still burned. Dennis lay asleep beside her. The house was full of creaks and scratching sounds from the wind outside.

Alice turned over in bed and tried to go back to sleep. After a minute or so she rolled out of bed and began to move toward the bathroom.

She was near the bedroom door when it swung open, hitting her shoulder. She gasped and jumped backward.

A man's voice said, "Who the hell's this? Goldilocks?"

Alice pulled a blanket off the bed and wrapped it around herself. "Dennis," she said. "Wake up!"

Dennis mumbled. He stirred and rubbed his eyes. Finally he propped himself up on his elbows. "Christ," he said. He looked at the man. "Hi, Rawly," he said.

"I usually don't ask questions," the man said. His Southern accent was heavy. "But right now I can think of a few." He was a short man, nearly bald, wearing jeans and cowboy boots.

"I thought this was Neal's room," Dennis said.

"You thought wrong." The man looked from Dennis to Alice and back to Dennis again. "Why don't you get dressed and come on downstairs. We'll figure it out over a beer."

He went away.

Alice immediately pulled on her clothes. "You didn't say he was a southerner," she said.

Dennis buttoned his shirt. "He just talks that way," he said. "He was probably born in Bridgeport."

When they came downstairs Rawlings was nowhere in sight. A woman with long, red hair lay on the sofa. "Hey," she said to them, her voice lazy.

Rawlings came in from the kitchen, carrying a six-pack of beer by its plastic webbing. "This here's Molly," he said, handing a beer to the woman on the sofa. "This here's Goldilocks."

"Alice," Alice said, her voice thin.

Rawlings tossed a can of beer to Dennis, who flung out his hands and managed to catch it.

"Budge down," Rawlings said to Molly. He sat next to her on the sofa.

Dennis pointed to a rocking chair next to the fireplace. Alice sank into it. Dennis sat on the carpet.

Rawlings took a long swallow of beer. "My my," he said. "What'd you all do in here? Have a barbecue?"

"Sorry about the smoke," Dennis said. He sneezed.

"Bless y'all," Molly said.

"It was my fault," Alice said. "I forgot to open the flue."

Rawlings laughed. "It smells kinda nice," he said.

Dennis opened his beer. A spume of foam hit his shirt and sprinkled the carpet. "My my," Rawlings said.

Molly set down her beer and belched audibly. "Listen to me," she said, giggling.

"We been to a party," Rawlings said.

Molly looked over at them and stopped giggling. "Dennis," she said, as if noticing him for the first time. "Dennis, Shelley called for you. She called this afternoon. She said it was urgent."

Dennis didn't meet Alice's eyes. He stood up. "Excuse me," he said, and went quickly into the kitchen.

"Lucky I remembered," Molly said.

"Yeah, yeah," Rawlings said. He looked over at Alice. Then he went to the stereo and lifted its cover. He took the Otis Redding record from the turntable and shook his head.

In the kitchen Dennis was saying, "Damn it, Shelley. What is it now?"

"You come from around here?" Rawlings said loudly. He grabbed a Dolly Parton album from the stack next to the stereo.

Dennis was saying, "Okay, honey. Okay."

"No," Alice said, staring straight ahead. The can of beer felt like ice in her hand. "No. I'm not from around here. Not me. I come from a million miles away."

Dog

Everyone seemed to know her. She passed the Donovans' house twice a day, holding the leash of a light grey terrier—a breed Dmitri had seen only once before, in a circus at Leningrad. She was a tall woman who walked from the waist, as a ballerina does.

She was quite punctual: she made her morning passage just after nine, and her evening appearance around six. She always wore gloves, and a brown leather purse hung from the wrist of the hand that held the leash.

"That's Mrs. Edward Woodruff," Mrs. Donovan told Dmitri when he asked. Then she cleared her throat, as if she had swallowed the words that she wanted to say.

Dmitri watched for her every day. As she walked, her black hair floated behind her. She usually wore tailored suits, which seemed too constraining for one who walked with such vigor. She was meant to wear sheer summer dresses, and flowers in her hair.

The dog, a small fellow, had a rectangular head. His eyes seemed full of intelligence. He strutted alongside the woman as if he wore no leash, as if he owned her.

Tonight she wore a coat made of some dark fur, and she seemed to walk more briskly than usual. She must be a wealthy woman to afford such a fur, and the night must be a cold one, Dmitri thought. He had not been outside since his arrival here, in accordance with the Donovans' rule that he "lay low a while."

He saw the woman's hair whip in the wind, and he imagined the smell of the air outside—burning leaves, perhaps, or wood smoke, mingled with salt from the sea, which they told him lay less than a mile distant. It struck him that, despite the leash, the dog was a freer and happier fellow than he!

Dmitri had met the Donovans after his "escape"—that was how he thought of it now. He had slipped away after a recital at Carnegie Hall. At a restaurant nearby, he said to a waiter one word: "Asylum." The waiter was too busy to help. But Dmitri persisted. In the end he had to shout before the manager was called.

The police came and took Dmitri away. Two days later, after answering a stream of questions posed by men dressed in tweeds like English gentlemen, Dmitri was brought to the Donovans.

And two weeks later, here he was—restless, uncertain, and homesick for friends he would likely never see again.

Dmitri noted his emotions with peculiar clarity, as he noticed everything during this time—the Donovans, and the autumn weather, and the street itself, with its wide lawns and oddly designed houses that looked Spanish, or English, or French.

He asked Mrs. Donovan about the variety of architecture, but she clearly was not interested. "Finish your dinner," she told him. Dinner always began at seven. She pressed upon him caviar, blintzes, and borscht, which she said came "out of a can." None of the food tasted familiar.

"You will make me fat!" he said, holding up his hands.

"Never!" Mrs. Donovan said. She pinched his cheek. "You're a skinny thing without any color," she told him. "You can't even grow a beard on what you eat."

His beard was blond, scarcely visible. He blushed. He glanced at the photograph of Mrs. Donovan's son that stood on the fireplace mantle. From the photograph, the son seemed a heavyset man in his early thirties, with a fierce smile. He would have no trouble growing a beard, that fellow!

After dinner Dmitri walked again to the window, thinking of the woman with the dog. And a minute or two later, as if summoned by his thoughts, the woman appeared. Wrapped in her fur, she stalked past, fallen leaves blowing around her. Just as she walked out of sight, the dog stopped and turned back. He pulled his mistress behind him as he trotted into the Donovans' yard, toward the bush that Mr. Donovan called "my poor forsythia." As the animal lifted his left rear leg, the woman looked up, straight into Dmitri's window.

Startled, Dmitri backed away for an instant; then he caught himself and boldly stepped forward again. The woman looked worried. Dmitri smiled. He waved. The woman smiled back and shrugged, holding both hands toward him, gloved palms upward.

The dog ignored them.

*   *   *

At eleven the next morning his hostess brought in a platter of buttered toast and a bowl of pâté. Dmitri was at the piano. When he stopped playing, she asked the name of the music. "Piano Concerto No. 1," Dmitri told her. "Tchaikovsky."

Mrs. Donovan pointed to the tray of food. "Appetizers," she said. She urged him to have some vodka. When he declined, she poured a glass for herself.

"Mrs. Woodruff wants to meet you," Mrs. Donovan said, setting her glass on the polished surface of the baby grand piano. "You know. The lady with the dog."

Dmitri looked from the pâté to his hostess. "She wants to meet me," he said. "It is safe?"

Mrs. Donovan poured more vodka into her glass, spilling a few drops on the piano. "Safe enough," she said. "Her husband is a spook, too."

"Please, can you explain?" he said. It was the phrase he always used when his English failed him.

"Edward Woodruff works for the government, just as my husband did before he retired," Mrs. Donovan said. "We're all friends here." She smiled, her mouth stretched thin.

Dmitri wondered why Mrs. Donovan disliked the woman with the dog.

*   *   *

Mrs. Donovan loaned him a sweater that had belonged to her son. "Keep it," she said. "Brian owns a third of Manhattan now—he won't miss an old jersey."

The sweater was hand-knit, with a thick cable stitch. Dmitri spent several minutes arranging its collar to his satisfaction and brushing his short blond hair. Could it be thinning already? His uncles in Yalta were bald, every one of them. The thought of those uncles made him sad. Whenever would they meet again?

When he came downstairs, he heard a strange voice, low-pitched, intermingled with those of his host and hostess in the place they called the living room. Then—it happened too quickly—he joined them, saw her eyes widen as Mrs. Donovan introduced them. She took his hand. Later she repeated her name when he asked. "Celeste Woodruff," she said, adding quickly, "Edward couldn't get away."

He realized that he was smiling too much. Mrs. Donovan handed him a glass.

Celeste. She had wonderful eyes—light brown, the color of honey. And her voice was dark, legato. "You must be bored here, waiting for things to be settled," she said to him. "How do you pass your days?"

"I practice," he said. "At the piano. That is why I come here. To play."

The others smiled.

"Edward's not involved in this Beirut business, I hope," Mrs. Donovan said.

Mr. Donovan cleared his throat.

"I have no idea," Celeste said, her eyes darting from face to face. She shifted her drink from one hand to the other, so that the ice made a ghostly sound against the glass. "I'm never able to keep it straight," she said, looking at Dmitri as if confiding in him alone. "He's in Turkey, he's in London, he's in Bombay. Who knows where he is tonight?" She laughed, but Dmitri thought that her laughter sounded forced.

Mr. Donovan gripped her elbow, and they all walked into the dining room. Four places had been set at a long table with room for twenty or more.

"You're here, ducks," Mrs. Donovan told Dmitri, pulling out the chair on her right.

Celeste sat across from him. The candlelight glinted on the fine hairs along her forearms. She wore a dress made of some thin, soft material that might be transparent in brighter light.

She and Mr. Donovan talked about the theater. They said it was a poor season—the worst in his memory, Mr. Donovan said. Of course there was one play from England.

Mrs. Donovan said that the English play was a dud. As they debated the merits of the play, Dmitri contemplated Celeste. Her eyes were lively as they moved from his host to his hostess, and her face had a fine, high color. She might be any age from twenty to forty, he thought. American women were hard to judge; the faces of Europeans revealed so much more.

Celeste looked at him, her hands twisting a crescent-shaped crust of bread. "It must be odd for you, coming to terms with this new place," she said. "What do you miss most?"

Without thinking, he said, "The sea. I am liking the sound of it always. At night, at home, it is my lullaby." He liked that word. "Lullaby," he repeated.

"Pardon?" Celeste's lips, stained the color of brandy, pressed together and curved.

"Yes, I'd like another," Mrs. Donovan said, handing her glass to her husband. "Dmitri was saying that he missed the sea," she said in a firm voice to Celeste, as if she were translating.

"But hasn't he seen it?" Celeste turned back to Dmitri. "We are only minutes away from the Sound," she said, speaking slowly. "I will drive you down there myself some afternoon."

"We can do that," Mrs. Donovan was saying, but Dmitri nodded and smiled at Celeste. "It is safe, no?" he said.

Mrs. Donovan raised her eyebrows.

"It is safe," Celeste said, reaching across the table to touch his arm. "You are in America now."

*   *   *

Celeste wore small gold earrings shaped like seashells. He felt giddy as he slid into the leather seat of her car. It was his first outing, and like someone venturing out after a long illness, he felt the world come rushing back to him. The car made a wonderful sound as they drove. She wore brown leather gloves. He watched her hand move from the steering wheel to the gear stick.

The dog sat across her lap. When Dmitri had entered the car, the dog turned to inspect him briefly. Then, as if bored, the dog turned around again.

No one else was at the beach on such a bleak autumn day. They left the car in an empty parking lot. Celeste led the way over a sand dune. The dog trotted behind.

As they crested the dune, he tried to mask his disappointment. As far as he could see, the water stretched in an unbroken grey line. There was no surf, no sound except for the gulls crying as they circled overhead.

And the sand looked dirty.

"What is it, Dmitri?" She had pulled the collar of her coat around her face, and she seemed smaller here.

"It is different at home," he said.

"I'm sorry," she said.

"No, no," he said. "You are not to blame."

"I wanted to please you," she said.

"No," he said. "You have done well, to please me. Thank you for bringing me here."

She shrugged and jammed her hands into the pockets of her coat. Her lips puckered. It disarmed him to see so elegant a lady pout as a child might.

She moved away from him and stared out at the sea. After a time she turned back, and somewhat to his own surprise, he embraced her.

He stepped back. "Please forgive me," he said, but she pulled him into her arms again.

Dmitri had made love to a few girls on the beach at Yalta. Each time there was clumsiness, embarrassment at the nakedness; and everything had to happen fast, before someone could come upon them.

But Celeste was different. Calm and languorous, she bade him to remove his shoes. Later, and only once, he scanned the beach for signs of intruders. All he saw was the dog, lying nearby on the sand, his pink tongue indolent on his lower lip. When their eyes met, the dog stared until Dmitri, abashed, looked away.

*   *   *

As Celeste's car pulled into the driveway, Mrs. Donovan

emerged from behind the forsythia bush. She carried a pair of long-handled pruning shears. When Dmitri stepped out of the car, Mrs. Donovan rolled her eyes at him.

Celeste drove off without comment.

"Well, what do you think?" Mrs. Donovan asked him.

Confused, he glanced down to make sure his clothing was in order. He brushed sand from his jacket with both hands.

His hostess's shoulders seemed to droop. "I think I've made a total hash of it," she said.

Then he understood—she was speaking not of him, but of the forsythia bush.

* * *

And she was right, was his hostess, Dmitri thought later that evening, as he stood at the window of the music room. The bush, formerly full and somewhat symmetrical, had been mutilated; one whole side appeared to have been hacked away, while the other side straggled heavenward.

Mr. Donovan was away on some sort of business—a lucky thing, in Dmitri's opinion. At the best of times, his host was prone to black moods, most of them directed at, or inspired by, his wife.

"We'll dine tête à tête," Mrs. Donovan said, wheeling in a small cart loaded with food. She insisted on bringing most of his meals to the music room; rarely did they sit downstairs, in the formal dining room.

Mrs. Donovan plunged an ornate serving spoon into a casserole dish. "Goulash," she said.

Dmitri scarcely touched his food, although he drank glass after glass of red wine. He felt tired and foolish, and full of suspicions. Celeste had asked him silly questions about his life in Yalta. For all he knew, she might be a government agent, or just as bad, a guilty wife who would have him deported. He should have known better!

His hostess stared at his plate without comment. She seemed not so much hurt as sorrowful, but who could tell the reason? She made no mention of the food, nor of his outing with Celeste, nor of the mutilated forsythia. In truth it was a rather silent meal.

As Mrs. Donovan cleared away the plates, Dmitri resumed his place by the window. He knew Celeste was coming, he could feel her approach. Yet, when the small dog trotted into view, followed by his sleek mistress, Dmitri felt startled.

The dog made a beeline for the forsythia bush. Celeste gazed up at him, her face mysterious in the dim light.

Dmitri sighed, and placed his right hand over his heart.

*   *   *

The next day, the brown Corvette pulled in at noon. Dmitri, at the piano, heard its engine roar and then idle.

"Excuse me, please," he said to Mrs. Donovan, who was clearing away the remains of an early lunch. He ran lightly down the stairs.

In the front seat Celeste kissed him, then threw the car into gear. He did not ask where they were going.

"Where is the dog?" he said.

"Anton? He's at the vet's." She seemed pleased at his interest.

"Nothing wrong, I hope?" he said.

She grimaced. "Poor darling, he may have worms," she said. "Let's not discuss it. We'll pick him up later, and he'll be as good as new."

He repeated the words to himself: "Good as new." "I like America," he said suddenly.

"Well, thank God for that," Celeste said.

The car paused before a set of wrought-iron gates. Celeste pulled a gadget from the dashboard and pressed a button, and the gates swung open.

Dmitri turned to see the gates swing closed after the car passed through.

The house was enormous and white, with great pillars supporting a long veranda on its second story. But Celeste pulled the car past the front door without a sidelong glance. She turned off to the right, toward a small white cottage behind the big house, bordered by fir trees.

"This is my place," she said.

The wind was high, and he felt chilled by the time she had

unlocked the cottage's door. Inside, they climbed a carpeted flight of stairs that opened into a wood-panelled room.

"I should have come in earlier and turned the heat on," Celeste said, pulling her fur coat closely around her. She turned a metal disk set in the wall.

Dmitri bent to examine a vase of dead flowers on a table. "What are these?" he asked.

"Loosestrife, those are called," Celeste said. "They've been here since summer. I should throw them away." She stood there, hands in her coat pockets, looking at the flowers.

Dmitri moved toward the fireplace in the room's center wall. He went onto his hands and knees to look inside it.

"Brilliant," Celeste said. "There's wood in the closet."

Once the fire was lit, and Celeste brought in a bottle of brandy from the small kitchen, the place took on a bit of life. Celeste pulled an Oriental carpet and a pile of cushions nearer to the fireplace, and they settled there, passing the brandy bottle between them.

"I probably shouldn't have come for you today," Celeste said, her eyes thoughtful. "I thought at the time that it wasn't the right move."

"But why?"

She smiled at him. "I should have played harder to get, you know."

He shook his head. He ran his fingers along the soft fur of her coat. "I don't understand."

"No," she said. "I don't believe you do understand."

Despite her smile, he sensed her unhappiness. He stretched out his fingers and lightly touched the fine skin above her eyes, noticing for the first time the small wrinkles there, the lines of age. Her coat slid from her shoulders, releasing as it fell the scent of narcissi and jonquils—the perfume she always wore. It was as if spring had come into the room.

Later, in the darkness of early evening, they drove to the veterinarian's to collect the dog. Anton sank into his mistress's lap with a dispirited air and would not look at Dmitri once during the drive back to the Donovans'.

*   *   *

After that day, their lovemaking began in earnest. She could make love for hours, this woman; she never seemed to be tired or fully satisfied. They spent nearly every afternoon in the upstairs room of the cottage. From time to time Dmitri would venture into the adjoining bathroom and see in the mirror above the sink his face, red and ravaged-looking, the face of a much older man.

Neither was she easily satisfied elsewhere. She found her car unreliable, her housekeeper uncivil, her hairdresser capable of malice. If Dmitri said something that displeased her, she would pout; the more he tried to explain, the more she would sulk. At such times he thought her an impossible creature. Sometimes, when she mispronounced his name ("Dimitri," she would say, and the sound of it infuriated him) or displayed her truly incredible ignorance of politics, he thought her stupid.

But the sadness in her eyes was real, and it made her moods and minor failings only seem poignant to him. And so he took on the challenge, the eternal challenge, of trying to please her.

She spoke of her husband rarely, and then only as "he." "He'll be away another week," she would say. Or, "I must stay in tomorrow afternoon. He's phoning at three."

Sometimes Dmitri gazed from the cottage windows at the great silent house across the driveway, wondering if anyone were ever at home there. Celeste never invited him inside, and in truth he did not want to see the rooms she inhabited with her husband.

*   *   *

One afternoon without warning, Dmitri had a fit of melancholy as they lay in their usual place, covered by her fur coat, before the fire.

Celeste stretched across him to reach a copper-colored box of chocolates. She chose one and bit into it quickly. "Nasty!" she said, returning the chocolate to its box.

Then she turned to Dmitri. "What is it? What's the matter? Tell me," she insisted, until at last he said, "What will we do when your husband returns?"

"Nothing will happen," she said. "We'll just go on hold for a while."

"On hold?" The words made him suspicious.

"We won't be able to meet, obviously." She spoke slowly, as if she were thinking hard. "And then he will be gone again, and we'll see each other."

Dmitri shook his head. At this moment she seemed to him shallow, without feeling.

"What is it?" she asked again.

"You act as if these things mean nothing," he said. "Your betrayal of your husband, your lovemaking with me."

"Betrayal?" she said. "That's a good one, coming from you."

He threw off the fur coat and began to pull on his clothes. She wrapped the fur more closely around her.

"Betrayal," she said, her voice low. "As if it were possible to betray that *apparatnik.*"

The word startled him. "Sorry?"

She repeated it. "You ought to know that word, it's Russian."

"Do you mean *apparatchik?*" Dmitri corrected her pronunciation. "But it is not possible. Your husband is a member of the Communist Party?"

After a moment, she began to laugh. She laughed so hard that finally he laughed, too. She reached for his hand. And on the strength of their laughter, they made love again.

*   *   *

One morning Dmitri awoke and the world outside was white with snow. Like a child he dressed hurriedly and ran downstairs, past an amused Mrs. Donovan, and stood outside, head tipped back to catch the wet snowflakes on his tongue.

He was thus engaged when a voice bade him good morning. He looked around, but the speaker apparently had walked on, past the house. All he saw was the back of a man, muffled in hat, scarf, and overcoat, pulling behind him a leash, at the end of which gambolled Celeste's dog.

Anton paused to shake a paw, as if he disliked the snow. He must have seen Dmitri, but he made no sign of recognition.

*   *   *

Then the waiting ended. Mr. Donovan told him that the arrangements for his future were well in hand. Within a year he would be eligible for a green card, the badge of a resident alien. And whenever he chose, he could leave Long Island.

Privately, Mrs. Donovan let him know that such long delays did not always follow a Russian's defection. A cousin of Dmitri's who worked in the KGB had presented certain problems, she said.

But those matters apparently were resolved, for the Donovans helped him find an apartment in Manhattan and arranged for furniture and a piano.

Throughout this time, Mr. Edward Woodruff remained at his residence. Dmitri heard nothing from Celeste. Once he saw her walking Anton, and he ran down to join them. But she spoke to him only briefly, her eyes on the windows of the Donovans' house (as if those windows had been blind before and now, with her husband's return, their vision had been restored!)

She said they must not meet. "He's suspicious, darling, he can tell that I've been up to something," she said.

He tried to tell her his news. "I will move into the city soon," he said. "We can meet there."

Already she was walking away. "I'll call you, darling," she said.

"No!" He shouted after her. "Not like this!"

But Celeste never looked back. Her dog did, briefly, as if intrigued by the spectacle of Dmitri shouting in the snow, without benefit of overcoat.

When Dmitri went inside, Mrs. Donovan was waiting. Wordlessly she put her arms around him. "It probably won't help," she said, "but you should know this—she did the same thing to my son."

*   *   *

Soon afterward, Dmitri moved into Manhattan. The streets and shops were bedecked with tinsel. He had Christmas dinner with the Donovans, and spent New Year's Eve at a party given in honor of an aging and much-beloved French singer. He had been introduced to a circle of musicians and dancers, and they made him welcome in a world that seemed to him entirely artificial.

In February, he was invited to join the orchestra of a ballet company for its production of *Petrushka*. He began to work seriously, building his days around long hours of practice. He had never been at home with Stravinsky, whom he thought less an innovator than a caustic critic; nonetheless, he was determined to rise to the challenge of those exasperating arpeggios.

In the evenings, he drank with friends. Things were not so bad. But, although he told no one about Celeste, he thought of her every day, remembering the details of her person: the delicate skin around her eyes, the shape of her breasts, the fine hair along her forearms, the sound of her laughter.

During this time it occurred to him that, in leaving Russia, he had left also himself—that while he lived in Russia, concealing much of what he felt and thought, and depending on only a few close friends for understanding, he nonetheless was his truest, most honest self. The new and glorious life of which he then had dreamed now seemed tawdry, facile, stupidly complicated—infinitely poorer stuff. This "free man" he had become, what use was he to himself or to anyone?

He met an assortment of American women. Many of them seemed to find him attractive. But when he was with them, he made comparisons, unspeakable ones. Over time he developed a secret contempt for any woman who was easily satisfied. He felt that for the first time he was coming to understand women, and the fundamental baseness of their nature. Indeed, he might have become a complete misanthrope, had he not decided to attend the opera one evening in early April.

His decision was an impulsive one, prompted by a cancelled dinner engagement. He purchased one of the least expensive seats. He told himself that he did not want to see *Prince Igor,* only to hear it.

As usual, the music captivated him. He lapsed into a state hardly approximating normal consciousness. At the intermission he roused himself, and made his way toward the bar.

He bought a glass of wine. Then he turned and saw her. She stood near a potted tree of some kind. Her hair was pulled back, revealing her neck. She wore a dark red dress. Her elbow was bent, her long fingers wrapped around a plastic drinking cup. Next to her stood a florid-faced man with grey hair, dressed in a grey dinner jacket. *Apparatchik* indeed!

He watched them, as if waiting for a revelation. They did not speak to each other. They merely stood, watching the crowd, sipping from their plastic cups.

Dmitri began to make his way toward them. He lost sight of them for a time as the crowd shifted. When his view cleared, he saw to his surprise that Celeste stood alone.

She did not see him until he placed his hand upon her shoulder. Then she turned, and her face seemed to contract at the sight of him.

"Good evening," he said.

"Dmitri," she said, elongating the first syllable in the old way.

At the sound of her voice he felt sorrow in his heart. "I love you," he said.

"Oh, God," she said. "He's just gone to the men's room. He'll be back any moment." She added, "I've missed you so."

"Please, Celeste," he said.

"Go now," she said. "He's coming back! I'll call you tomorrow."

"You must promise to call me," he said.

"I will. I do! I'll call you tomorrow, my darling."

He touched her hand. Then he turned and went back to his seat. He watched the aisles, waiting for them to return, but he must have missed them in the crowd.

Then just before the lights dimmed, he saw them, two heads in a row far ahead of his. He admired her hair and, when she turned, the shape of her ears, small and perfect as seashells.

Her husband's head seemed squarely set on a neck as thick as Celeste's waist!

For the rest of the evening he watched only those heads, silhouetted against a vibrant and ever-changing background.

*   *   *

So it began again. She telephoned him the next day and spent the following weekend at his apartment. Her husband left for England. Soon she was spending three or four days a week with Dmitri.

His work suffered, but he scarcely noticed. *Petrushka* was behind him. He played nothing but a little Schumann. An agent had booked his concert tour for the following season, but there was plenty of time to prepare. Summer had not yet begun.

From time to time he and Celeste talked about the future. She must leave her husband, Dmitri said. But Celeste did not like change. She found the marriage convenient, and since her husband was no trouble to her, why bother to leave him?

"I can love you just as well this way," she told Dmitri. "Frankly, being married has nothing to do with love."

Dmitri did not agree. But they had so little time together, and the future, as such, seemed very far away. For the time being, he lost himself in trying to please her. When she left his apartment, she always left behind some possession—cosmetics, a nightgown, stockings. Then she began to leave more substantial things—clothes, shoes, and even, one memorable weekend, her beloved dog.

She was off to spend the weekend with her parents in New Jersey, she told him. Her mother had been ill, and even when well, did not get on with Anton.

"I think she actually may be jealous of Anton, of my feelings for him," Celeste said. "Can you imagine?"

Dmitri's relations with the dog had never progressed beyond mutual mistrust. But he welcomed Anton's presence as one more sign of Celeste's growing attachment to him. Soon, he felt sure, she would move in herself, once and for all.

So Dmitri found himself, twice a day, circling his block on the east side of Manhattan. The dog trailed behind him as far as possible, as if they were not together at all.

Dmitri had never paid much attention to the animal's habits. He had thought the white terrier who sat on his mistress's lap a fairly clean little fellow. This opinion now was sharply reversed. He watched Anton slink through the city streets, putting his nose into trash cans and curbside refuse, lifting his leg at grossly inopportune moments, and drooling continually.

"You are disgusting!" he told the animal more than once.

But Anton, it was clear, did not care what Dmitri thought.

They spent a quiet weekend, nonetheless. Anton slept while Dmitri played Schumann's *Fantasie,* and they dined on chicken casserole.

*   *   *

On Sunday the weather was sunny and hot, the first spring day to presage summer.

Dmitri found the day unexpectedly pleasant, and rather than return to the apartment after buying a newspaper, he decided to take a longer than usual walk around the city.

The dog seemed to sense Dmitri's mood. Instead of his customary disinterested shuffle, Anton broke into a near sprint. Dmitri found himself breathing hard after six or seven blocks and tried to slow the animal's pace. But Anton had the lead today and pressed on regardless.

At last, and to Dmitri's chagrin, the dog paused to relieve himself—in a gutter directly opposite one of the city's finer hotels. Dmitri averted his gaze. He was peaceably watching the fluttering of flags over the hotel entrance, when he saw her.

She looked elegant, wearing a new spring coat, coming down the carpeted steps that connected the hotel to the street. She walked arm in arm with a young man—a man younger than Dmitri! She smiled, and the young man smiled. She bent her head to listen to him.

Dmitri felt as if a flame were shooting from his belly through his chest, through his heart. He slowly clenched his fists.

Was it then that he dropped the leash? Afterward he could not remember the sequence.

All that he retained were images, scarcely connected: the white flash of fur as the terrier darted into the street; the kaleidoscope of cars suddenly frozen; the mild curiosity on the faces of the handsome couple leaving the hotel as they heard the squeal of brakes; and finally, the face of his mistress when at last she saw him, and their eyes met and held steady, over the confusion that lay everywhere between them.

As Good As It Gets

Thursday night when we finished work, Angela and I headed for her place. We walked six blocks more than we had to, just to stay away from the river, and the air smelled good to us after our eight hours inside. The streets were slick with summer rain. Even the carbon monoxide smelled fresh. Some jerk in a truck rolled down his window and shouted "Babes!" at us. We ignored him, but after the truck was gone we smiled at each other.

"Face it, we're gorgeous," Angela said. "We're the best thing in town."

Angela and I work in insurance claims, in an office without any windows. We spend our days processing words on computers and opening other people's mail. We generate piles and piles of paper that no one will look at again—until a policyholder sues the company. Once I saw a television show about life at the bottom of the ocean. Life at the office is something like that—dim and quiet. All the sounds, even the telephones, are muted. But you get the sense that far away, enormous things are moving through the darkness, colliding from time to time.

The sidewalks downtown were deserted. Sometimes I think Angela and I are the only two adults left in this city who don't own cars. In the old days we would have stopped at O'Brady's. But two years ago the city council passed an ordinance banning happy hours. Now, when people finish work, they put on their raincoats and go home.

Usually it rains here. In the winter we get the state's most significant snowfall. All year round it's humid. The unemployment rate is high, and the divorce rate probably is higher. Get the picture? I've lived here all my life. You can ask me anything.

Tonight we walked out of downtown (called "Business District" on the road signs) and hurried through the rundown residential section. From nearly every house we passed came television sounds—gunshots or artificial laughter.

Angela has an apartment on Canada Street—yes, Canada Street, named for our neighbor just across the border to the north. This town has a reputation for being anti-Canadian, something to do with our balance of trade and their moaning about the acid rain we cause. We take their business, they pollute our river, and acid rain keeps on falling, nobody knows why. Anyway, poor old Angela is stuck on this little cul-de-sac called Canada Street, and when she tells people where she lives they say "Where?"

When we got there we had a few beers and Angela boiled us up some spaghetti. After we ate, we sat in her living room, complaining about the usual things—money, clothes, men. We never talk about work.

As I was saying good-night, Angela's phone rang. I waved myself out and on down the stairs.

But she called after me: "Marlene, hold on. We're going rock and rolling tonight."

I came back up. "We are?" I said. "Where?"

She said "Yeah, you too," and hung up the phone.

"Big night at O'Brady's," she said to me. "Sixties Night."

"What?"

"A very special event," she said. "Tonight only, at O'Brady's Bar and Grill. We wear sixties clothes. We dance and drink. We meet many beautiful men."

"At O'Brady's?" I hadn't been there since the last happy hour. In fact, I hadn't been to any bars since my so-called marriage broke up. "I'm too old for that stuff," I said. I'm pushing thirty. Angela's twenty-four, pushing forty.

"I'm too old for this stuff." Angela mimicked my voice. "Hear me, Lord! Take me now, Jesus!"

"Take yourself," I said. Since the divorce I had had exactly two dates. The first was with a guy from our office who confessed that he liked to eat mayonnaise on toast and that every day after work he watched "MASH" reruns. On week-ends he watched "MASH" reruns on tape. That was all. That was everything about him. My second date was with a sensitive type who talked about the poetry of ordinary life. He bought me a hamburger. In the car going home he tried to maul me with one hand as he drove, all the while telling me why local real estate was going to boom.

"The best part of these special events," Angela was saying, "is getting dressed up."

From her closet she pulled an old flowered shirt. She found a pair of fuchsia shorts in her bureau. Next she pulled on black ankle socks. She handed me an old plaid skirt that was much too short, and a tight red sweater, and black tights with have-a-nice-day faces printed on them. We argued over who would wear her white tennis shoes. She won, and I stayed in my black go-to-work pumps.

Angela ponytailed her hair, which is the color of corn silk, and brushed mascara on the punked-out bits at the front until they looked like black spikes. "The thorns of my crown," she said, using her special vampire voice. It always thrills me when she uses that voice to answer the phone at work.

Then we did our faces in white powder, black eye shadow, and dark red lipstick—just like those bimbo models in the Robert Palmer video. "You think Robert Palmer is Canadian?" I asked Angela, while I moussed back my hair.

She was phoning a cab. "Nah," she said. "He's a Brit."

"Big difference," I said. We watched our reflections in the window as we waited for the cab. "I'm not sure we look like the sixties," I said.

Angela shrugged.

"Who's going to turn out on a Thursday night at O'Brady's?"

"Everyone," Angela said, yawning.

And she was right. They all turned out, from my hotshot dentist to Angela's ex-sister-in-law to every third office worker you see gobbling lunch downtown by the War Memorial fountain.

The parking lot was jammed. We got out of the cab and sniffed the river stench for a moment to get our bearings before we went inside.

A guy in a sharkskin suit stood at the door. "Far out," he said when he saw us. "Real cool." But he made it clear that we had to pay him five bucks to get in. "Band tonight," he said. He hit our palms with a red stamp that left imprints like fresh wounds.

We walked inside. O'Brady's hadn't changed since happy hour days. The walls were panelled with plastic-coated pine, and customers had scrawled their initials right through the plastic. The tables were topped with yellowing formica, personalized by cigarette burns. All around us people milled in near darkness. Several stared at us, and we stared back. Women in beehive hairdos were wearing full skirts with poodles on them. Men with slicked-back hair had on letter sweaters and chinos. The jukebox was playing early Elvis.

"Something's funny about this," I said to Angela. "Are you sure it's Sixties Night?"

"Fifties, sixties, what's the difference?" she said. "I like him." She pointed at a tall, dark man wearing Wayfarer sunglasses and a jacket that read "PURPLE GHOSTS MARCHING BAND."

"That's an actual school band, I believe," I said. I would have said more, but Angela gave me her zombie look—especially effective tonight, with the black rings drawn around her eyes—and pushed me to the other side of the room.

"George MacPhearson," she whispered. I eyed the spot we'd been occupying and there he was. George is a big-deal photographer from Toronto. He free-lances the annual reports for our office. He's sixty, though he says he's fifty-four, and a miserable lecher to boot. Don't ask how I know.

Tonight he wore a white suit and green suede shoes, and he was talking to a sinister-looking teenager in red. "And you think *you're* too old for this place," Angela said to me.

We brushed past a pool table where a couple of Elvis look-alikes were shooting eight ball. Then we got caught up in a mob headed for the bar.

O'Brady's bar is L-shaped and altogether must be forty feet long. Every inch of it was occupied tonight, but Angela squeezed her way in.

"Two beers," Angela ordered.

"You got proof?" the bartender asked.

"Proof of what?" she said. "Proof that I exist? Proof that you don't?"

"Just show him your card," I said.

Angela flashed her much-worn sheriff's ID, and we got our beers. It was hard to drink them. Every time I raised my glass my elbow collided with the back of the woman next to me—a woman all in black, with a killer hairdo as high and stiff as cotton candy. I smiled politely at her. She glared at me and I glared back.

Angela said, "Hi, Miss Wood," and pulled me away.

"Miss Wood?" Then it hit me. "You mean Miss Wood our high school guidance counselor?"

"The same," Angela said.

"Here?"

"Why not?" Angela said. "Someday I got to talk to that woman."

"Yeah," I said. "Ask her how you ended up in a two-room apartment on Canada Street."

Somebody must have pulled the plug on the jukebox then, because "Heartbreak Hotel" died just as Elvis was doing the second chorus, singing about how lonely he was. People were turning toward the stage that runs across the back of the barroom. On it a man in a white shirt was shouting into a microphone. "WELCOME TO FIFTIES NIGHT," he said. "O'BRADY'S IS PROUD TO BRING YOU THE BEST IN LOCAL ENTERTAINMENT." And so on.

Finally the man on stage went away and on came the band—four guys wearing skinny pants and ducktail haircuts. From the way they held their guitars I guessed they held daytime jobs as auto mechanics. They played "La Bamba." The lead singer obviously didn't know the words—he mashed a lot of Spanish-sounding syllables together—and he wasn't even good-looking.

"This seems about right," I said. All the people around us were ugly, although a few had risen to this occasion. A baby-faced woman wore an enormous dress with a pillow stuffed up the front. On her chest she had pinned a button that read "I SUPPORT LINCOLN HIGH ATHLETICS." She danced with a guy in a football uniform, clasping his hand, moving across the floor in slow twirls.

I spotted my dentist, standing alone and smiling at no one in particular, but he looked away as if he didn't know me. "I should go over there and open my mouth at him," I told Angela. She shrugged.

"What's he doing here anyway?" she said.

"He's here to support the arts," I said. "Like you and me."

We returned to the bar just in time for the evening's two-for-one drink specials. For one dollar we received two glasses of liquid, the color of which varied from brown to orange.

"Is there vodka in this?" I asked.

"It's spiked with LSD." The guy standing next to us bared his teeth.

"How do you know what's in it?" Angela said.

"I made it." He had short red hair that stood straight up and glistened with hair spray.

"Made the drinks or the acid?" Angela said. She took a sip, and her mouth curled.

"Ah, a detective," He held up his wrists. "Take me away," he said.

I gulped down the drink, ready to leave. But Angela did not move.

Her way of taking men on was quicker than anything I could manage. I took my drink and walked through the crowd. A few minutes later, a tall greaser-type in a leather jacket asked me to dance.

"Why not," I said.

Once we began to dance, we kept at it, pounding away on the floor for half an hour or more. The band was playing Elvis songs. I hadn't danced in years, not since my ex-husband "escorted" me to a volunteer firemen's ball and—don't even ask.

From time to time I tried to figure out if this fellow was good-looking. The room was too dark for me to be sure.

One thing I did know. This guy could dance. He had on

oil-encrusted Levis that fit him like latex, and he moved *fast,* which suited me. The music and the drink were so awful, and the place smelled like ten thousand years' worth of stale beer and cigarettes. The only escape was to lose ourselves in the dancing. And we did.

After a while the band launched into a number made famous by the Everly Brothers. My dance partner suddenly held up one hand and walked away from me. I tried to figure out what he meant. Maybe he couldn't dance to anything but old Elvis songs. Then a little smiling man came over and said, "May I have the honor?"

Against my better judgment I followed him across the floor. But I kept an eye out for the greaser-type all the way through "Bye Bye Love" and "Wake Up Little Susie." And at last he appeared at the edge of the dancing, zipping his fly as he walked. He headed straight for us. He put one hand on my shoulder and looked down at my partner. "Bye-bye," he said.

"See you!" I called, and kept dancing. When I looked again, he was gone, and the greaser was everywhere, gyrating like a madman. The band broke into "Rave On," one of my favorite Buddy Holly songs, and bad as they were, the music sounded good to me. My partner and I danced in a small, tight circle around each other, twisting, spinning, turning our backs on each other from time to time. The band didn't stop when it shifted into "Not Fade Away." Neither did we.

Finally the lead singer garbled something into the mike, and the band left the stage. Immediately the lights came up. For the first time all night we could see each other. I blinked and looked across at my partner and—lo and behold—I had struck it lucky. He had beautiful eyes, long tilted eyes like a cat's, and the rest—all that grease and hair—were merely special effects.

He put his hand on my arm. "Hey gorgeous," he said.

We hit the bar again for one last beer. Angela was nowhere to be seen, but I didn't worry about it.

My greaser said nothing more. The head of a snake was tattooed on his left hand. Its body twined up his inner arm. On his right arm he wore a medical ID bracelet, but I couldn't identify the emblem of his ailment.

The end of the evening hustle was on at the bar. People who had arrived alone were making a last desperate search for someone to go home with. There was plenty to watch, all of it predictable.

The greaser touched my arm. His touch felt, you might say, electric. And when he motioned toward the door with his long, cool eyes, I floated right beside him.

Outside, the parking lot was alive with activity, just as it was back in my high school days. People were drinking and smoking non-tobacco substances. You could hear women laughing in the cars.

I noticed a foot in a familiar white tennis shoe dangling from the window of a Sentra. Meanwhile, the greaser led me to a Datsun parked nearby. He unlocked the passenger door and I got in. I wondered where we were going but knew that if I asked, the spell would be broken.

He sat behind the steering wheel and reached into the back seat for a paper bag. He pulled out a bottle of whiskey—the kind they advertise on billboards around here—and offered me a swig. I shook my head.

He raised the bottle in a silent toast. We sat there, watching the action in the parking lot. Somewhere people were singing what might be an alma mater or might be something obscene. Three or four guys threw a phosphorescent Frisbee over the cars. I could no longer see Angela's foot. I rolled down my window and turned to look for it. The Sentra was gone.

I took a deep breath. All I could smell was the river.

"I don't want to know your name," the greaser said then.

I shook my head. "No," I said. "That's the magic of it."

"We probably will never see each other again," he said, each word separately striking the night air. "It's like a story I read." He took a swig from the bottle. "Two people meet. There's something between them. It's not lust. It isn't love either. It's something else."

"What is it?" I asked.

"Passion," he said. "Some pure emotion. They decide to

let it live for one night only. Then, to keep it pure forever, they end it. They never see each other again."

It occurred to me that I had read something like this myself, back in high school English class. But in the book I read, the woman didn't fall for it.

"Have you ever done this before?" I asked him. Not that it mattered much.

"Of course not," he said.

"Forgive me for asking," I said. He brushed his hand across the back of my neck.

Then we climbed into the back seat.

* * *

I asked him to drop me off at Angela's place. I didn't want to go home dressed as I was. I live in a slightly respectable neighborhood.

Angela was either out or asleep, I figured, so I let myself in with the key she keeps under the flowerpot. But she was standing in the kitchen, eating cold spaghetti. I sat her down and, after a little prompting, told her what I've told you.

"God, it's unreal, Marlene," she said. "Promising to keep your passion pure forever. It's like something that happened to somebody's grandmother."

I sat on the edge of the table, feeling dizzy. The Axl Rose poster on the wall seemed to watch me contemptuously.

"And you don't even know his name?" she said. "You'll never see him again?"

I shook my head.

She looked woebegone suddenly, sitting there in her old flannel nightgown with streaks of black still around her eyes. "So much for romance," she said.

"Cheer up," I told her. "It could be worse."

For a minute or so we looked at the floor. Then she began to moan. It seems the guy with the Sentra was, get this, from Kitchener, Ontario. "He called me Angel," she said.

I mimicked the voice of a local deejay: "Second prize, *two* weeks in Ottawa."

"Heaven help us," Angela said. Although we hardly believe in heaven. Or angels, for that matter. We believe in stuff like cancer and television. Stuff that you know is really out there. Stuff you can count on.

"So you've fallen for one of our neighbors to the north," I said. "After everything I told you about my ex."

"They can't all be like your ex, Marlene," Angela said.

I could tell from her face that she didn't understand. So I kept quiet. She rattled on about the Canadian boyfriend, what he said and what she said, and what to make of the kiddie car-seat she had seen in the back of his Sentra.

"Maybe the car-seat belongs to his sister," I said. My voice sounded hollow from lack of sleep. I cupped my hand over one ear so I could hear myself better and said it again: "Maybe the car-seat belongs—"

"Shut up," Angela said.

But after a while she said all right, I could sleep on the sofa. She made room for me there, along with the mangy stuffed animals and the secondhand quilts. It wasn't as cold as I had thought it would be.

Yet I couldn't sleep. I lay there, counting wrinkles in the ceiling. Everything was green from the glow of Angela's Gumby night-light. Then I lost count of the wrinkles and I got depressed. From time to time I have moods. What a joke, I thought. You work to get money so you can buy stuff that breaks down or gets used up or bores you. Then you work to buy more. In between, you watch television. If you're lucky, you go to parties. Maybe you end up in the back seat. Pretty soon, you die.

When I get these moods, the only thing to do is let my mind spin and spin until it winds down, like the drum of a clothes-dryer. And then I go to sleep.

I went to sleep. And I dreamed, of all things, about dolphins. There were hundreds of these animals, sleek and shining in the moonlight, swimming up the river and nudging against the rocks along the riverbank. People came down from the city and stood along the bank to watch them. Some of the men carried children, and the women stood with their arms folded, and they talked to the dolphins as if they knew them. And the dolphins answered them.

I wasn't there. I wasn't in my own dream! But I felt happy

about all of it just the same. It was all very quiet, that dream. It was, you know, sort of civilized.

I woke up suddenly, not sure where I was. The night-light had burnt out, and the room swam in grey light from the street. Angela was snoring. I knew that what I had dreamed was impossible. After a moment, I began to cry. Angela didn't wake up, for which I was grateful.

But in the morning, when Angela did wake up, she made me see things differently. She made me realize that it hadn't been such a bad night after all. She reminded me that both of us had certainly known far worse.

Everything we had said and done could be blamed on the drinks, she said—the drinks and the stars. Our horoscopes for the previous day were both full of warnings. Our ruling planets all lay in unfortunate conjunctions. There was no use crying over spilt milk.

And if we ever ran across those particular two men again, we would simply act as if we had never seen them before.

Besides, she said, didn't I know what day it was? It was Friday. Directly ahead of us, here it came—a whole new untouched weekend.

I listened. I did not interrupt. I paid attention to everything that she said. We had instant coffee for breakfast, with a shot of rum in each cup for luck.

Then we headed out, back to the office again.